L... ...T FOR WOMEN WHO
GO GUNNING FOR LAWMEN...

"I think she likes you, Longarm. She asked me
who you was and described you as that nice-looking stud. Ain't that a bitch?" Pop said.

Longarm said he was swearing off women, for a
true one could seldom be found. He brought the
older lawman up to date on his misadventure with
the Spooky Widow Harris. Pop found the tale
amusing and agreed that any sheriff worth his salt
would surely trick a confession out of such a predictably unpredictable sass. "I'd say you was ahead,
Longarm, you accounted for at least one gun who
was trying to stop you from getting here," said the
old lawman.

Longarm said, "Yeah. Now if only I can figure out
who sicced all them *other* guns on me..."

TABOR EVANS

IN NO MAN'S LAND

A JOVE BOOK

LONGARM IN NO MAN'S LAND

A Jove Book / published by arrangement with
the author

PRINTING HISTORY
Jove edition / September 1983

All rights reserved.
Copyright © 1983 by Jove Publications, Inc.
This book may not be reproduced in whole or in part,
by mimeograph or any other means, without permission.
For information address: The Berkley Publishing Group,
200 Madison Avenue, New York, N.Y. 10016.

ISBN: 0-515-06259-6

Jove books are published by The Berkley Publishing Group,
200 Madison Avenue, New York, N.Y. 10016. The words
"A JOVE BOOK" and the "J" with sunburst are trademarks
belonging to Jove Publications, Inc.

PRINTED IN THE UNITED STATES OF AMERICA

Chapter 1

Longarm had often heard it said that no man with a lick of sense would ever shoot craps on an army blanket, insult the mother of a man who had the drop on him, or try to serve wanted papers on anyone riding for the Rocking X—unless he took along at least a full troop of the U.S. Cavalry to back his play. Trying to pinch a Rocking X rider solo was not considered asking for trouble. Those who knew the outfit called it just plain suicide.

Nonetheless, when Longarm learned that the Rocking X had trailed a herd up to Denver from the Panhandle and was currently camped along the South Platte just outside of town, he didn't see that he had much choice. His informants had said the Rocking X had sold its beef in the Burlington Yards and would be heading home as soon as they could round up their riders from the various Denver places of ill repute and get them all sober enough to travel. So Longarm hired a mount from the livery nearest the federal building and proceeded to do some traveling in their direction alone. He didn't think of it as showing off. He had a job to do. Things sometimes happened that way when a man packed a badge for a living.

It was just after noon and the Denver city limits lay a wistful few miles behind him when Longarm spied the cow camp where his informants had said he would. Blue smoke rose above the cottonwood and crackwillow lining the bank of the wide, shallow river beyond. The ponies of the remuda were tethered upstream, grazing peaceably. Wilder and woollier looking critters were hunkered about a cow-chip fire near the chuckwagon.

The riders for the Rocking X had a reputation to keep up, but some of them were dressed just plain silly. One old boy wore woolly chaps and another wore fancy batwings. Half of them sported Texas ten-gallons big enough for a family of Indians to live in, and more than one looked Indian. Longarm knew that the Rocking X hired hands off the nearby Indian Nation to the south.

As they saw him riding in, a couple of the hands stood up, but most of the dozen-odd hardcases just went on inhaling coffee and smoke as though they didn't see him. An old geezer in a cook's apron turned from the chuckwagon's tail gate with a pot of Arbuckle in one hand and the other hand resting thoughtfully on the grips of an ancient Walker Colt he wore under the apron.

Longarm tended to make lots of folks thoughtful when they first sized him up. He sat mighty tall for a man riding such a short horse. The tobacco-colored tweed suit and shoestring tie they made him wear in Denver didn't look as towny on Longarm as it might have on some. His pancaked Stetson was set cavalry style and his face was tanned dark enough to pass for a breed. He'd left his Winchester at home, not wanting to seem surly, but the grips of his crossdraw .44 peeked out from under his frock coat as he reined in at serious shooting distance and dismounted.

The cook had the rank on the dollar-a-day hands present,

so Longarm smiled at him as he led his pony the rest of the way. He held the reins in his left hand. The cook said, "The boss ain't here, but I can tell you we ain't hiring. You're too late for grub, but I'll be proud to coffee you afore you ride on, stranger."

The others who had risen sat back down as Longarm tethered his mount to the spokes of the chuckwagon's front wheel. It wasn't for them to say if the tall stranger joined them for coffee or not. Longarm took the tin cup of Arbuckle in his left hand, but remained on his feet as he told the cook, "I thank you kindly, and I mean to drink it all. But to tell you true, I was hoping to find the Richardson boys here."

The cook didn't answer. One of the hands spoke up. "Old Tex Richardson stayed back on the home spread this trip. His brother, Reb, ramrodded us north. He should be back from town directly."

As Longarm nodded down at him, a denim-clad and darker individual at his side growled, "You sure talk a lot for a Cherokee, boy!"

The Cherokee shrugged. "Hell, the man asked polite," he replied in a defensive tone, "and it ain't like the boss is on a secret mission."

Longarm addressed them both, smiling thinly. "To spare us all a certain tingle in the air, gents, I know the Richardson boys and they know me. I go by the name of Custis Long, and the first time I met up with old Tex and Reb was when the three of us were riding drag for Captain Goodnight, just after the War."

Cherokee smiled and said, "See, Osage? I told you the man was polite."

Osage—if that was his name—stared up at Longarm with Apache-black eyes and didn't answer.

"Which side did you ride for in the war," the cook asked, "and what business do you have with Reb?"

Longarm took a sip of Arbuckle. "I disremember every detail of the War. As to what I want with Reb, I'll tell him when I see him."

3

There came a low, collective growl as everyone waited to see what the cook would do about such an answer. The cook studied his options, then shrugged, picked up some pots, and wandered over to the river bank to scour them with wet sand. Old camp cooks were supposed to be tough. On the other hand, one good way to get old enough to matter was to know when to back off. Longarm saw that the only man in camp with the power to start any serious trouble had decided not to, so he hunkered down with the others as Cherokee murmured to Osage, "Cooky's scairt! Ain't that somethin'?"

The surly Indian growled, "Jesus, you have a big mouth for a man with no brains. Nobody's scairt. Cooky's waiting on the boss to decide it one way or t'other, you halfbreed idjet."

He was staring hard and unfriendly at Longarm as he spoke. Longarm met his glare, unwinking, with his own gunmetal gray eyes. "I know some Osage folk over in the Nation," Longarm said. "They're named Tallchief. Any kin of yours?"

Osage shook his head. "I know them. Not well enough to matter one way or the other."

"Do tell. The Osage Strip ain't all that big. No offense, but are you a pure-blood Osage?"

The Indian blinked, frowned, and demanded, "Are you trying to start up with me, mister? You'd better be good with that double-action under your coat if you're hinting at *Creek* blood in my family, hear?"

"Now, don't get your bowels in an uproar, old son. I know Osage and Cherokee don't mix enough to matter with Creeks, for some reason." He took another sip of coffee and added innocently, "I just thought I saw a little Berdachee in your handsome features, is all."

Cherokee laughed, and Osage looked bewildered. Osage shot Cherokee a dirty look, then shook his head at Longarm. "Hear me, I am pure Osage to the bone," he insisted. "We men of the civilized tribes live white. But none of the women

4

of my family sold their flesh to white men for beads, like some Cherokee I could mention."

Cherokee laughed again and said, "He's just jealous 'cause he ain't as pretty as me. Everybody knows my grandmammy's tribe had the handsomest squaws to begin with."

Longarm nodded at the whiter youth. Aside from his wild and woolly outfit, Cherokee could easily pass for a dark-skinned white boy. Longarm knew it was true that of all the tribes of the Nation, the Cherokee had the most white blood. That was partly because, as Cherokee had said, the women of his tribe had looked more like a white man's notion of pretty to begin with. But mostly it was because the Cherokee had started back East and had been the first tribe to adopt white ways and establish friendly relations with their white neighbors. "I know some of *your* tribesmen, too," Longarm said, "Over near Fort Smith. The Starr family. Any kin of yours, Cherokee?"

He shook his head. "Nope. My last name's Arrowsmith."

Before he could elaborate, Osage interrupted. "I have been thinking. I thought I knew every tribe in the Nation. What was that one you just mentioned?"

"Berdachee? I reckon I might have called that wrong. They're generally found more to the north, Osage. I meant it friendly. Berdachee are said to be mighty handsome. But you'd know best if you had any on your family tree."

Another unsmiling hand who could have been Indian, too, spoke up. "Boss is riding in."

Everyone stood up—the hands to be polite and Longarm to feel safer. He saw the cook coming back from the river. He wasn't surprised.

Reb Richardson reined in at the edge of camp but sat his mount to study some as he spotted Longarm. Of the two rebellious Richardson boys, Reb was the older and meaner. He was almost as tall as Longarm and twice as broad across the gut. He didn't have to dress wildly to look tough, so he just wore denims and a sensible Stetson. Anyone within a country mile could see Reb figured he was in charge of everything and everybody in range of the two guns he wore low, in a border buscadero rig.

Longarm put his tin cup on the chuckwagon's tool box and strode to meet the boss. Richardson knew the man on the ground had the advantage at close pistol range, so he dismounted fast and tossed the reins to a willing hand. He faced Longarm soberly and said, "Afternoon, Longarm. I surely hope you have a sensible reason for pestering my boys."

Longarm held out his hand to shake, saw Richardson didn't want to, and dropped it, keeping his own voice polite. "Before you get your bowels in an uproar, Reb, I'll say up front that I take very little notice of beef unless it's missing from a federal herd. I hope you got a good price in town for your herd, however accumulated?"

"I did. The price of beef has riz up here. That's how come we trailed our beef this far north, this summer, instead of running it over to the the Panhandle and Santa Fe yards in Amarillo, as usual."

"I figured you had a good reason, Reb. But that's between you and the state of Texas. To save a lot of spittin' and whittlin', Reb, I'll say right out why I'm here.

"You know who I work for. A short spell back, a federal agent was gunned by a gent named Bob White. I doubt that was his real name, of course. We have a very poor description of Bob White. But we know he was last seen leaving the Indian Nation suddenly, and headed for the Panhandle. We know you and your brother were the only outfit in the market for new trail drivers. Most of your neighbors down that way won't be rounding up until later in the fall. So—"

"Hold on," Reb cut in. "Are you hinting one of my riders might be the man you hold a want on, Longarm?"

Longarm shook his head. "I ain't hinting, Reb. I'm saying. I know you have a mighty paternal attitude about the boys who work for you. But before you cloud up and rain all over me, let's study on our bound duties. I don't like to call a grown man a liar, so I'll not ask you which of these

6

boys you hired recently. I don't think you or your brother would be dumb enough to hire a man who'd put 'wanted for murder' on his job application, neither. So, when you study on it, you might not owe Bob White as much as I can see you think you do by the look in your big blue eyes."

Reb Richardson was too slick to glance at any particular member of the innocently staring assembly around them. He said flatly, "You're way off base on the Rocking X, Longarm. I give you my word as a Confederate officer that the man you want can't be here. I heard about that land management man getting kilt down in No Man's Land. Me and the boys was rounding up beef nigh a hundred miles south at the time, and we can prove it if you want to wire Amarillo. We had a mighty tedious discussion with a pesky brand inspector about the time that federal man was kilt. So it don't matter when I hired anyone in this crew. They all got ironclad excuses, and you can tell your copper's narks I said so!"

It was Longarm's turn to look confused. "Back up and run that by me a second time, Reb. I never said anything about a land management man getting gunned."

"Sure you did, damn it. You just said you was after a breed for killing a federal agent, didn't you?"

"I did, but we seem to have one left over. I hadn't even heard about a killing in No Man's Land. The affair I'm working on concerns a dead Indian agent. It happened over a month ago, up north on the Pine Ridge Reserve. Bob White was living on the Sioux agency, either as a squaw man or a relative. Like I said, we have a poor description on him. White got into a fight at the trading post over unpaid bills. When the smoke cleared the Indian trader and the agency man who'd come in to bust up the fight lay dead on the floor. The murder warrant's made out on the agent. Folks who trade with unreconstructed Sioux know what chances they're taking in business. And, what the hell, how many times can you hang one killer? At any rate, after shooting up the trading post, White lit out for the Indian Nation. He'd told some Sioux drinking buddies he had a

7

gal down there. By the time some deputies from Fort Smith could get over to her spread, he'd beat her up because they were out of booze, and lit out for Texas, as I said. So, you see, we're back where we started, Reb."

Richardson said nothing.

Longarm said, "Let's be sensible about this, old son. We're talking about an ugly drunk who beats up women and tells fibs when he asks for a job punching cows. I know better than to hope you'd stand still for me arresting one of your regular riders. But the cuss I'm after hasn't ridden for you two paydays. Am I right?"

Reb Richardson shrugged. "Well, I've seen the valley and I've seen the hill. It's been a good life, so far, and I surely would have liked to kiss some more pretty gals. But you ain't taking in one of my regular hands, Longarm."

Longarm nodded, seeing light at the end of the tunnel even as the big boss saved his face by only opening the door a crack. "I came with no such intent, Reb," Longarm said. "Can I take it you and the boys won't act silly if I only take a rascal who just started riding with you under false pretenses?"

Reb Richardson smiled crookedly and replied, "If you can. None of us will help either way, and you'd surely better pick the right man. I can't remember just who I might have hired last."

Longarm nodded, reached under his frock coat to unfasten the handcuffs from the back of his gunbelt, and turned to Cherokee with a grim smile. "Hold out your hands or fill 'em with hardware, Bob White," he said. "For I don't give a shit either way, and I'm taking you in, dead or alive, for the murder of Agent Hawkins on the Rosebud Reserve."

Cherokee did neither. His eyes got big and he called out weakly, "Boss?"

Reb Richardson shrugged. "The man said you could slap leather if you aimed to, kid. It ain't my deal. I never turnt you in."

Cherokee hesitated, choked, and held his hands out mutely. As Longarm cuffed them together, Reb Richardson asked, conversationally, "How did you *do* that, Longarm? Was it them woolly chaps?"

Longarm pocketed the key to the cuffs. "Nope, lots of old boys dress wild," he said. "I knew this was Bob White before you rode in. I waited politely before I pinched him, knowing you'd want some explanations, Reb."

"That's for damned sure. All right, you picked out the one man who just signed on. But I'd take it kindly if you would tell me how. I'd hate to think one of my other hands ratted on anyone who's ever drunk my Arbuckle."

Longarm smiled. "Hardly any of 'em said word one to me, Reb. You got 'em well trained. The only gents a man could get a polite word out of was yonder cook, old Osage, and this bitty skunk, here."

"I said nothing!" Osage protested with a scowl.

Longarm said, "Sure you did, Osage. I asked if you might be a Berdachee, and you said you'd never heard of such a tribe. White, here, laughed. But not another man in camp so much as cracked a smile. Tell him what a Berdachee is, White."

"Don't let him have me, Osage!" the prisoner said. "We've rid together, and this son of a bitch calt you a Berdachee!"

Everyone else still looked blank. "Berdachee is Lakota for a mighty swishy Indian boy," Longarm said. "None of you gents from the Nation talk Lakota. Only this rascal laughed when I implied a hardcase like Osage dressed up girlish and gave pleasure to unwed braves. Old White, here, not only talks Lakota, he don't know shit about the Cherokee Strip if he never heard of the Starr family. But, then, he only stayed there long enough to beat up a squaw. I'll need the loan of a pony for this rascal, Reb. I'll see it's returned to you, of course."

Richardson said, "Go to hell. You couldn't even have *him,* if he'd told me right off he was wanted by the law."

"Would you have hired him anyway, Reb?"

"Don't go fishing into who might or might not be on my payroll. Take Cherokee out of my sight afore I change my mind."

Longarm nodded and moved the prisoner toward his tethered mount. "Well, Denver ain't that far, and the walk will doubtless settle your nerves some," he said.

But as Longarm untethered his mount, Reb Richardson asked, "Longarm?"

"Yeah, Reb?"

"Just between you and me, who do you reckon would have won, had you guessed wrong?"

Longarm smiled softly. "I reckon we'll just have to guess, for now, Reb. I like to kiss gals, too. So it likely turned out mighty lucky for at least one of us."

"I still think I could take you if I had to."

"Well, Reb, let's hope you never feel you have to. I ain't as curious a cuss as you, and the outcome figures to be a mite permanent for the loser."

Chapter 2

The following morning, Longarm shocked everyone at the federal building by getting to work on time. It couldn't be helped. It had been too close to payday for serious drinking the night before, and that infernal pretty widow woman on Sherman Avenue had guests from back East visiting and said she had to consider her reputation.

Getting to the office on time didn't mean that he beat his boss to work. Nobody ever got there ahead of U.S. Marshal Billy Vail. He was seated behind his desk, already going over the papers piled on the green blotter, when Longarm ambled in, sat down in the leather guest chair across from him, and lit a cheroot without comment.

The older, pudgier Marshal Vail shot a glance at the banjo clock on the oak-paneled wall, blinked in mild surprise, and regarded Longarm thoughtfully from under his bushy brows. "I can see you ain't sick, and if you're building character for an advance on your salary, forget it," he told his deputy.

Longarm exhaled a cloud of smoke and replied, "I'm sure pleased to find you in such a sunny mood this morning, Billy."

Vail grinned despite himself. "As a matter of fact, I am. I already thanked you proper for bringing that killer in yesterday afternoon. I'm feeling mighty slick about what *I* done, after. I got him singing like a mockingbird with a hot poker up its ass last night, while you were out getting in trouble as usual."

"I didn't have the wherewithal to get in much trouble, boss. How did you get him to sing so fine? While I was marching him into Denver on foot I got the distinct impression he was feeling silent and surly."

Vail said, "That's 'cause you was holding a gun on him and making him trudge dust on a hot day. Last night, after he'd simmered in his cell a spell, I dropped by, saying I was his court-appointed lawyer."

Longarm blew a thoughtful smoke ring. "Is that allowed, Billy?" he asked. "Seems to me a U. S. Marshal acting as someone else might be sort of dirty pool."

Vail snorted in disgust. "Now, where in the Constitution does it say a lawman has to play fair with a damned old murdering breed? The son of a bitch will get a fair trial afore we hang him. Meanwhile, as I said, I introduced myself as a mighty slick lawyer who could mayhaps get him off with life if he came clean with me. So he did, and now I've got a whole mess of unsolved cases off the infernal books."

"I'm proud of you, Billy. I do so hate untidy files. And, what the hell, they can only hang him once. While you were hanging every possible crime you aimed to solve easy on the skunk, did you get him to confess to that killing I told you about down in No Man's Land?"

"No, and it's the *Unassigned Strip* to Washington, even if No Man's Land sounds less sissy. The rascal had an alibi for that one, and he even alibied the rest of the Rocking

12

X—for murder, leastways—when he confessed they were all stealing cows farther south at the time."

"I wondered why Texas beef was getting sold so far north. Want me to follow up on that, Billy? Reb Richardson sort of issued me an invite to see who was the best man."

Vail shook his head. "Forget it. The beef's been sold and we can't do every damn chore for the Rangers. Texas is supposed to watch its own damn beef." He rummaged through his papers, found a memo, and said, "Here's your next case. Land office down the hall didn't know one of their agents was gunned, or even missing, until I asked them about it this morning. I'm sending you down to the government-owned Unassigned Strip to find out what happened to who, when, and where."

"That's a mighty big stretch of empty to search, Billy. There must be three thousand sections of nothing much but open range to hunt wild geese in! If the land office ain't missing anyone, the whole tale may be nothing but a rumour. Did the prisoner tell you that anyone he knew had actually seen such a killing?"

"No, but everyone down that way was talking about it, so something must have happened. Here, take a look at this wire."

Longarm reached for the yellow sheet and scanned it soberly. He handed it back, saying, "All right, a gent from Ohio named Latimer ain't been heard from for some time. So what?"

"Hiram Latimer is the name of a gent who works for the Office of Land Management. Add it up."

"I just did, and it still don't make sense. Land Management says it ain't missing anyone, Billy."

"Pay attention to your elders, damn it. Hiram Latimer works out of the Denver office, down the hall. They ain't reported him missing because he ain't due back for a couple of weeks or more. He was sent to collect range fees and nobody gives a damn about whether he did or didn't get the checks until around the fifteenth of September, which ain't due for a spell. Meanwhile, he was reporting more regular to his kin in Ohio. When mail stopped coming, they reported him missing. Latimer was sending support payments for a kid of his back East. So they was naturally more interested in his keeping in touch than the folks he works for."

Longarm nodded thoughtfully and said, "Yeah, Latimer could add up to a missing land agent the land office hasn't been keeping track of. I didn't know the government collected range fees in No Man's Land, Billy, Come to study on it, I've never figured out how that big hunk of range got left out of any state or territory like it did. It don't make much sense on the survey maps."

Vail shrugged. "It was before your time, when the books was still kept sloppy out here. You see, just before the War, when the western states and territories was first getting surveyed, said survey teams had a lot on their minds besides careful mapping. The friction between North and South was coming to a boil. The Kiowa and Comanche were raising ned and lifting hair to the south. The State of Texas got an early start and claimed its current boundaries before the War. The Indian Nation to the northeast of Texas had been laid out by Washington. Meanwhile, Kansas was not called Bleeding Kansas for nothing. Guerrillas on both sides tended to jump most anybody they found alone on the prairie. So anyone running a survey line tended to run it simple and sudden."

"Colorado was still part of Kansas in them days, right?"

"Yeah, up to just before the War, when the Yankees wanted a couple of extra abolitionist state senators and granted separate statehood to the western end of Kansas. Forget the history of Kansas and Colorado. The point is that the gents running the survey line between the Indian Nation and Kansas run it arrow-straight, due west, claiming everything north of the line for Kansas and leaving everything south of said line to anyone left over. They guessed right on the Indian Nation's north border. When they got west as far as the Indian Nation went, on the hundredth parallel, they just kept going, assuming everything south of them was the Texas Panhandle. Remember, nobody was there to tell 'em

14

any different. They were surveying across empty, open prairie. They had such Texas maps as Texas saw fit to issue to the damn Yankees, so it was easy enough to miss the fact that Texas ended forty miles short.

"The rest is history. Kansas and Colorado were laid out square and neat. Nobody in Texas was ranging that far north in them days, so a slice of range forty-odd miles wide and damn near two hundred miles long was simply *left out*. Nobody noticed till after the War, when things got more civilized out here.

"As to where federal range fees come in, No Man's Land has never been claimed by any state or territory, but that ain't saying Uncle Sam is about to let all that grass be eaten *free!* You can call the strip No Man's Land, but *Uncle Sam* still owns it, and it's administered as federal open range. Hiram Latimer went down to collect grazing fees, and he's either dead or missing. Do I have to draw the rest on a blackboard for you, damn it?"

Longarm looked for an ashtray, didn't see one, and flicked the ashes on the rug discreetly. He said, "I'm on my way as soon as we solve a few sticky details, boss. I don't have the money for a train ticket in the first place, and I don't have the first notion where to get off in No Man's Land even if I did. Are there any towns at all in the disputed territory?"

Vail shook his head. "Not even a homestead, legal. Washington's held back on granting homestead permits until they can figure out what on earth they'll do with the property in the end. Texas says they'd be proud to add it to their Panhandle, but Texas was on the losing side in the War. And, while President Hayes has about wound up the Reconstruction, he's in no mood to give the losing side anything extra. Folks are talking about making the Indian Nation a full state, now that almost all of the civilized tribes can read, and some of them even got to church regular. Colorado and Kansas haven't shown much interest. So if they ever get that so-called state of Oklahoma going, it may wind up with its own panhandle. Meanwhile, the land's just sitting there, held in trust by Uncle Sam. There ain't no towns, since nobody's supposed to be living there till future notice."

Longarm frowned. "Hell, Billy, you just said the government's demanding range fees for the grass down there. Who's grazing it, if nobody lives there?"

"Folks who *don't* live there, of course. The strip's only forty miles wide, and as open range, anyone's allowed to cross it. The Rocking X just did—both ways. I don't think we'd best ask about any grass they may have used in passing. As I get it from my opposite number down the hall in the land office, they're only interested in spreads that run their cows on the range regular. You want to meet up with 'em and work out the details?"

Longarm shook his head and said, "Don't need to, just yet. I can see how it works now. Like most cattle outfits, spreads north and south of No Man's Land just claim a quarter section or so of taxable watered land and run their cows off across open range as far as they dare."

He took another drag on his cheroot and mused aloud. "Latimer wouldn't have looked for much out in the *middle* of nowheres much. He'd have been visiting outfits north and south of that forty-mile-wide strip. I'm starting to feel better about the job, Billy. A while back, I got in a lot of trouble with gun-toting owlhoots out in the middle of the strip. Empty places on the official maps tend to draw such critters the way flypaper draws the nicer pests. But if I only have to poke up and down around the edges, it shouldn't take all that long."

He flicked more ash on the rug. "That brings us on to the other problem. I don't have five whole dollars in the world. Of course, if I'm to be working out of the office, on an expense account..."

Vail sighed and said, "All right. I'll have Henry, out in the front office, issue you some cash vouchers along with your travel orders. But if you spend dollar one on another double room in a fine hotel, you can give your soul to Jesus, for your ass will belong to me!"

Longarm just smiled as he blew another smoke ring. "I

16

mean it, damn it," Vail grumbled. "You can't hardly get there from here. The Burlington for Fort Worth will drop you off at Trinidad, less than a hundred miles from the west end of No Man's Land."

"I'll borrow some cow ponies and a comfortable stock saddle from my pals at the Diamond K, then. May as well dress cow, too, since I'll want to do some serious riding without scaring folks on the open prairie in this scarecrow outfit you make me wear in town. Ain't there no closer railroad connections, Billy?"

Vail thought for a moment. "The Rock Island Pacific has a line running across the empty strip. It's even further out of your way, though. The tracks run across about midway between each end, and no trains stop there, for obvious reasons. I'm hoping you'll find out what happened to Latimer without having to ride the whole length, since he was last seen just south of the Colorado line. Are you sure you don't want to talk to his boss in the land office?"

Longarm nodded and got to his feet, saying, "May as well. I don't even know what the cuss looks like—dead or alive."

Billy Vail rose and led him out, pausing in the front office to tell the prissy youth playing the typewriting machine about the documents he wanted for Longarm by noon.

They found a prettier typewriter in the reception room of the land office down the hall. She was about twenty, had a pencil stuck in the bun of her dishwater hair, and said they'd just missed Mr. Waterford, her boss. She added that she thought he'd gone to the bank on a personal errand.

Longarm looked at the clock on the wall behind her. "If I was a boss, I doubt I'd come back before lunchtime, either," he said. "To save us some time, miss, do you know this Latimer gent everyone's asking about?"

The dishwater blonde nodded. "Of course. Mr. Latimer reports in every month or so. He's out in the field most of the time, but I've met him several times. He seems a sweet old dear."

"That don't describe him in much detail, ma'am."

17

"Oh, you want to know what he *looks* like? Let me see. He's about forty, I guess. Average height and build. Come to think of it, he's sort of average all over. His hair is brown. So are his eyes, I think. He's a bit old for my taste, but I suppose some women would find him attractive. There's nothing wrong or odd about his features. He wears a business suit except when he's out in the field."

"Have you ever seen him dressed to dun cows for back payments on grass, ma'am?"

"Let me see . . . Oh, I do remember him coming in here dressed like a cowboy one time. It was rather shocking. He's usually so neat. He had on those leather things they wear over their pants. He needed a shave, and . . . well, I don't want to cause trouble."

Longarm and Vail exchanged glances. Vail nodded and said, "We're asking about a man who may have been murdered, ma'am. This is no time to hold back on information, if you follow my drift."

She paled and nodded. "All right," she said, "he'd been drinking. He needed a shave and he smelled like he hadn't bathed since crawling out of a bottle. Mr. Waterford gave him a good scolding, too."

"Was that the last time you saw him?" Longarm asked.

The girl shook her head. "No. The last time he was here, about a month ago, he was all right. He was clean-shaven and well dressed. He apologized for the way he'd acted that one time, about—oh, a year ago. As I said, he's a rather sweet old dear most of the time."

They thanked her and stepped out into the hall.

"We could wait for Waterford, if you think that was important," Vail said.

Longarm shook his head. "It's tedious waiting for a boss who don't have to punch a clock. I'd say old Latimer had a periodic drinking problem. Why hang around for his boss to tell us he read him the riot act and got him to take the pledge?"

Vail said, "If he fell off the wagon out in the field, it could sure explain a lot. But we're not about to find him here in Denver, drunk or sober, dead or alive. Let's see if Henry has you set to leave yet."

"You go ahead, Billy. I'll come by just before noon and pick 'em up."

Vail frowned. "You'll do no such thing, Longarm. I know they serve a fine needled beer at the Parthenon just down the street, but the government frowns on such doings during business hours."

"Hell, Billy, do I look all that thirsty?" Longarm protested. "I told you I had to borrow some riding stock at the Diamond K, and there's barely time to make it there and back before noon."

Vail grumped away on his stumpy legs as Longarm grinned and went downstairs. There was no way in hell a man could get out to the Diamond K and back before noon. So he'd do it later, after he had a few schooners of needled beer just down the street.

Chapter 3

Trinidad, Colorado was an awful place to get off a train, but Longarm and the two ponies he'd borrowed from the Diamond K had no choice. The only small mercy was that the sun had set by the time the Burlington freight dropped them off in the Trinidad yards. Longarm had argued his way aboard with a courtesy pass, his borrowed stock saddle, and his possibles. He rode in the caboose with the brakemen while the ponies enjoyed the comforts of an empty Texas-bound cattle car. Longarm saw no need to pester his office with the details of how he'd converted his passenger coach ride to a little jingling money. No bank would be open to cash an expense voucher for him at this hour, and a man had to plan ahead.

Longarm knew he was stuck there for the night. He put the ponies up in a livery near the freight yards, tipped the hostler a dime extra to lock up his saddle and possibles, but hung on to his Winchester .44-40 for now as he moseyed up to the main street to see if Trinidad could really look as bad as it smelled.

Even with the lights out, one could tell that Trinidad was a coal-mining town. It lay in the foothills of the Front Range and shipped high-sulfur coal for a living. There were piles of coal all about, and the dry, thin air was filled with its black, gritty dust. Longarm lit a cheroot in self-defense, but it didn't help much. He couldn't inhale on a cheroot that tasted like burning kitchen matches.

The street he walked down had no sidewalks. It was paved with crunchy cinder and powdered slate from the mines. The city fathers, if Trinidad had any, had not seen fit to install street lighting away from the main area. Just enough light spilled out of the miners' shacks along the path to keep Longarm from tripping over anything bigger than a dead horse if he watched his step. But he saw brighter lights up ahead and heard the tinkle of a badly tuned piano, so he kept going. He wasn't out to admire music just yet. He'd told Billy Vail he would wire as soon as he detrained at Trinidad, and the brakemen on the freight had told him there was a Western Union office near the depot. He'd have gotten off there if he'd come down on the passenger combo which was due in about half an hour.

He came to a corner that was about as lit up as anything in a coal-mining town ever got, and stopped to get his bearings. The awful piano playing was coming from the batwing doors of a corner saloon just to his north. He looked south and spied the gas lit sign of the all-night Western Union, with the bulkier form of the railroad depot looming beyond it. He headed that way, composing a night letter for his boss in his head as he walked. He didn't have a thing to tell Billy Vail that Billy didn't already know. It was a shame. You got to send longer messages cheaper by night letter.

He started to enter the Western Union office. Then he frowned and muttered, "You're getting old, pard. Billy's sure to have a copy of the Burlington time table, for he told you which train he expected you to be leaving on."

If he wired this early, the office would catch him in a harmless fib that hardly cost the taxpayers enough to matter. A night letter wouldn't get there before morning, but the sneaky Western Union rascals put the infernal time they'd recorded the message on the same hunk of yellow foolscap.

Longarm took out his watch, saw that the train he was supposed to have taken was due in about twenty minutes, and headed on to the depot to wait for it.

The waiting room was empty, the ticket window closed for the night. That made sense. In the unlikely event that anyone from Trinidad meant to go to Texas tonight, they could settle up with the conductor on board the next and last train.

He spied the door marked GENTS and went in. There was no attendant on duty. Longarm noticed there was a tub room down at the end of the row of urinals. At least, that was what the sign above the locked door said. It promised a hot bath with soap and a towel for two bits. If only the infernal man had been there to unlock it! Longarm had intended to take a bath before leaving Denver, but between one thing and more needled beer than he'd ever intened to have at the Parthenon, he'd barely returned from the Diamond K in time to catch his train. The ride down in the sooty caboose hadn't done wonders for him, either. He'd changed into denims and a hickory shirt to go out in the field, but his collar itched anyway, even loose.

He ambled down to the locked door to see how seriously they meant to keep him from having a quick scrub. It wasn't hard to pick such a sissy lock with a certain blade of his pen knife. He stepped inside and struck a match to light the oil lamp. The tub was there, but there was neither soap nor towels, and when he ran the hot tap, experimentally, the water came out coffee-brown and cold as a banker's heart. He shrugged. Hell, he didn't need a bath that bad.

He turned to leave, but he heard boot heels and the jingle of spur rowels. He shut the door quietly. He didn't feel up to explaining to a couple of fellows why he'd just broken

22

into an empty room. It made more sense to let them take their leaks and to leave after them, discreetly.

Longarm listened, feeling sheepish, as the two men outside peed a spell. One of them said, "Jesus, that feels good. How come I seem to have to piss ever' couple of minutes tonight, Jimbo? You reckon it's something I et? *You've* been leaking pretty good, too."

Another voice growled, "You know damn well why. Are you sure we're going to get paid in full for this job, Matt?"

"That's what the man said. A hundred each up front, and another two hundred each after. It's a mighty fair offer for a couple of minutes' work, Jimbo."

"Bullshit. Six hundred all told is slim pickings indeed for gunning a man with Longarm's reputation!"

"Oh, hell, we got reps, too. And the poor bastard ain't got a clue we'll be waiting for him here. Like I told you, the depot's always deserted this late at night, and the platform's dark outside. Come on, let's get stationed proper. Longarm's train will be in most any time now."

Longarm cursed silently as he heard their boot heels clumping away outside. The sons of bitches hadn't had the consideration to outline their ambush in full before leaving to set it up.

He snuffed his cheroot, put out the lamp, and cracked the door open as he considered his options. He didn't like any of them.

Staying put seemed safe but tedious. Cutting out the front door of the depot and running for the town law seemed not only sort of yellow but sort of dumb. He had no idea what either of the would-be assassins looked like, and he doubted even they would be dumb enough to own up to being hired killers if and when the town law got around to asking. Anyone with a lick of sense would sort of crawfish back from the depot when they heard a posse coming.

Besides, there wasn't time. Once the train arrived and they didn't see him climbing down off it, they'd leave the depot to look for him elsewhere. And they had the drop on him, twice, since he'd never know who they were until they slapped leather.

That one jasper wearing Texas spurs was a slight break. In a mining town this far north, only one man in a hundred might stomp down the main drag going jingle-jangle. But he couldn't gun a man for wearing noisy spurs. Any innocent cowhand could buy them in any hock shop west of the Big Muddy, and a lot did.

Longarm stared morosely through the narrow crack at the empty men's room. A pissing wonder wearing noisy spurs didn't strike him as a gent who'd been killing folks for a living long. The bastard he was really after was the one who'd hired them. Longarm tended to agree, in all modesty, that six hundred dollars was sort of tightwad for a man who wanted a top gun shot.

It added up two ways: some miserly rascal who didn't know the going rates, or a pro who'd contracted to kill a man with a rep and aimed to do it the safe way by recruiting a pair of not-too-bright drifters.

Longarm wasn't going to find out by standing here in the dark like an owl bird. He quietly levered a round into the chamber of his Winchester and stepped out, holding the carbine at low port as he crossed the tiles on the balls of his spurless, army-booted feet. Near the exit to the main waiting room, he reached up to trim the remaining lamp before cracking a far more dangerous door. The waiting room was empty. The gunslicks were out on the platform, and the train would be coming soon.

Longarm slipped out of the men's room and backed toward the front entrance, with the muzzle of his Winchester trained on the platform doorway. Nothing happened. He got outside to the main street and glanced up and down. Nobody was in sight at this end of the mighty dull main street of Trinidad.

He lowered the Winchester to his right side and debated which way to circle the depot. Knowing how he'd have done it, Longarm figured the gunslicks would be hunkered down in the shadows at either end of the platform running

24

the far length of the depot. He could likely get the drop on one of them by coming around the corner from behind. But he wanted them both, and no matter which one he grabbed, the other would be in a hell of a good position to back off into the blackness, shooting or not.

He heard a far-off lonesome whistle as the southbound combo crossed a grade north of town. He had to make up his mind pronto. The train would be here any minute, and...then what? What would *he* do if he'd been hired to ambush a man getting off a train and the rascal never showed?

On the far side of the depot, Matt and Jimbo were swallowing butterflies, on opposite ends of the wooden platform, as the headlight of the distant locomotive grew larger than the evening star. Matt had positioned himself between a baggage wagon and the depot's clapboard wall. Jimbo was covering the far end from behind a water-filled rain barrel. The train kept coming, and it was too late to back out of the deal now. Matt unbuttoned his Levi's and took a last quick leak, while Jimbo tucked the muzzle of his .45 under one elbow and wiped his sweaty gun hand dry on the front of his flannel shirt.

The southbound rolled in, hissing to a stop and sending a cloud of steam across the platform. The light from the coach windows illuminated the entire length of the platform, and the only people getting off were a couple of girls in Dolly Varden skirts. The girls didn't hang about to be picked up by anyone. They just entered the depot and headed for wherever they were bound.

The two gunslicks stared slack-jawed for a time. Then the train whistled and started rolling on to Texas, leaving the platform dark again, and deserted except for two mighty confused ambushers.

Matt called out. "Jimbo?" His partner broke cover. "Hold it down to a roar, damn it!" he whispered.

They joined forces in the middle of the platform by the waiting-room door.

"He never got off," Matt said. Jimbo holstered his pistol

25

with a sigh. "Tell me something I don't know. Tell me more 'bout the asshole who hired us. You know him, I don't."

Matt shrugged. "He's just a good ol' boy I rid with once, like I said. He said to call him Lefty. I disremember his real name. What do you reckon we ought to do now, Jimbo?"

"Shit, what *can* we do? It didn't work. Let's get outten here."

Longarm had heard enough. He kicked open the door of the blacked-out men's room and snapped, "Freeze!"

Matt was the one with the Texas spurs, and he still had his gun in his hand. So as he fired from the hip into the blackness where Longarm might have been if Longarm had been dumb, Longarm jackknifed him and sent him to the floor boards with a .44-40 round just over the belt buckle.

Jimbo tried to touch the ceiling with his scared fingers and yelled, "I give! I give! Don't shoot!"

Longarm stayed put, half sheltered by the doorjamb, until he was sure that Matt wasn't ever going to pester anyone again. Then he said, "Bring your hands down slow, unbuckle your gunbelt, then grab some more sky as you step clear of the results."

Jimbo was disarmed and against the wall when, as Longarm had expected, a couple of gents with copper stars on their vests burst in the front door, guns drawn. Longarm had thought to pin his own federal badge to the front of his shirt, of course, so the town lawmen pointed their guns at the right party and demanded some explanations.

Longarm said, "I'm Deputy U.S. Marshal Custis Long. Just passing through. These gents were expecting me on the train which just left. Lucky for me, I took an earlier one. You can do as you like with the one I just shot. This other one belongs to me."

The senior town constable said that sounded fair. He sent his partner out front to hold back the curious people who had been attracted by the sound of Longarm's carbine.

"We'll be proud to hold him in the town lockup for you, Deputy Long," he said. "Say, ain't you the one they calls Longarm?"

"I am. Old Jimbo, here, don't need a jail cell. Him and me is going for a stroll. Come on, Jimbo. You can put your hands down now."

"Uh, where you taking me, Deputy?"

"For a stroll, like I said. Out the far door to the tracks. I want to talk to you in private. These boys will see your partner's buried, stuffed, or whatever."

As he herded Jimbo out, one of the town lawmen called after them. "Hey, Longarm, after he tries to escape, you will drop by the coroner's to make a statement, won't you?"

Longarm called back that he knew the form and he wouldn't take long. He nudged Jimbo in the ribs. "Keep going. Drop down to the tracks and head across 'em into the dark."

"Please don't gun me, mister. I know it looks bad, but I swear I've never killed anyone afore."

"Shit, boy, you didn't kill anyone. You sure must be a lazy cuss. The price of beef is up this year, and anyone who ain't afraid of work can get a job that ain't as injurious to his health."

He looked around and saw they were out of sight of the illuminated depot. "Stop and turn around. Take out your wallet. Put such cash as you have in your britches and hand the rest to me."

Jimbo did as he was told. "Please don't kill me," he begged. "Hey, I feel like I got to take a crap."

"Shit your britches, then," Longarm growled, putting the wallet and any I.D. it contained in his own side pocket with his free hand as he held the muzzle of the Winchester against the frightened youth. He sniffed, chuckled, and said, "I see you took my advice. All right, kid. I was hoping to take the one who knew who'd hired you alive. But things happen that way sometimes. I got a few more questions to ask. I'd like an educated guess as to whether the rascal you boys were working for knew both of you or only your pard."

"Honest, mister, it was Matt set it all up. He talked me into it. He said an old boy he'd once rode with was willing to pay us each three hundred dollars for gunning a lawman as was after him. I never met the cuss, and he never met me. He answers to the name of Lefty."

"All right. He sounds like a left-handed cowhand or former cowhand. That ain't much to go on. Was the deal made here in Trinidad, or elsewhere?"

"Matt met him this afternoon, up to the Peacock Saloon, here in town. I was camped down the tracks at the time. Me and old Matt had been sort of drifting south from Montana along the Front Range, looking for work. You may be right about the price of beef this summer, but they ain't been hiring anywhere we asked."

"A picture is emerging from the mist. You both looked like saddle tramps. I wouldn't have hired you, either. You want some fatherly advice, boy? Go back East and get a job chopping cotton, as the Good Lord intended. You just ain't cut out to be a cowboy, and I hope you just learned that you make a piss-poor gunslick, too."

Jimbo's voice was scared and suspicious. He licked his lips. "What do you mean, go back East? Ain't I under arrest?"

"Hell, old son, I got better ways to earn my keep than to waste my time on such as yourself. It's been nice talking to you, Jimbo. I don't have to tell you what will happen if I ever see your ugly face west of the Big Muddy again, do I?"

"Don't shoot me! I know what you mean to do! I ain't trying to escape. You can't make me run so's you can gun me in the back."

"Oh, shit, you've been reading too many stories, boy. If I aimed to gun you I'd have done so by now. I don't need to make up fool excuses. I outrank every lawman for a country mile."

He nudged the muzzle of the Winchester harder against the frightened youth's ribs. "Go thou, then, and sin no more, as the Good Book says. I got more serious chores to tend to."

Jimbo didn't move, but the fool was pissing down his

leg. Longarm turned away in disgust and walked back to the main drag, avoiding the depot just in case.

As he stopped between lamp posts to get his bearings, he saw that there was still a crowd around the depot front. Gunplay had that effect in small towns. He crossed the street and approached the Western Union office innocently.

Inside, he greeted the night clerk, picked up a pencil stub, and proceeded to file a full report to Billy Vail, shading the facts some to make it seem as if he'd been on the right train. He took out Jimbo's wallet and added full identification, in the unlikely event that the punk was wanted somewhere serious. Billy Vail would read between the lines and agree to the "escape," knowing they could easily pick up such a worthless rascal any time. A wanted flier up and down the line suggesting a quick peek at the local hobo jungle would be enough to round the fool up.

Longarm wasn't being as generous as it might seem to old Jimbo. Trying him on an attempted murder charge when no murder had come even close would be a long and tedious chore for a lawman who was on more serious business. As it was, he had to fill out all sorts of fool papers on the one he'd gunned. Since President Hayes had instituted all that reform legislation in Washington, it was getting sort of hard to administer simple justice out here.

He handed the form to the clerk and told him to send it as a night letter, collect. The clerk nodded, scanned the signature, and said, "Hey, if you're Deputy Marshal Long, I got a wire for you. It came in just this afternoon. They must have knowed you'd be by, huh?"

Longarm nodded, took the telegram, and put it away to read later. The office was always sending him last-minute instructions, and they mostly told him to behave himself. He asked the clerk where the coroner's place might be, and went to get that chore over with.

It wasn't hard to find. There was a sign outside a yellow frame house just upslope and around the corner from the saloon that contained the badly tuned piano. It was still playing, and as Longarm passed he saw by the letters painted on the frosted glass front windows that this was the Peacock Saloon his temporary prisoner had mentioned. He wasn't about to go in there, no matter what they charged for drinks. The rascal who'd sent the hired guns after him knew what he looked like, and Longarm could hardly say the same for the so-called "Lefty." He'd have a talk with the local lawmen about any left-handed strangers they might have noticed, if there was time. He had to either ride out by moon glow or find a place to bed down where they didn't ask a man to register by his given name. Longarm hated to wake up to gunfire.

He climbed the steps of the county coroner's house and twisted the doorbell. A woman came to let him into the dimly lit front hall. "I've been expecting you," she said. "They told me about the killing at the depot. Let's talk about it in my office."

Longarm followed her, staring soberly at her rear view as he got used to the notion of a she-male coroner. It was a pure caution how many gals were taking jobs the Good Lord meant for men, these days. Old Virginia Woodhull and them other feminist writers had stirred things up confusing as hell since the War.

The lady coroner ushered him into a brightly lit office. As she circled around to sit at her rolltop desk, he got his first good look at her.

He had already noticed that she was built nicely. And she sure was only wearing a dressing gown. Her long, strawberry blonde hair was unpinned and hanging down free. She said, "Forgive my appearance. I was getting ready for bed when they rang my bell to tell me I could expect you."

He stared at her cameo profile. "You must be an early riser. Most folk don't turn in this early, ma'am."

She turned to face him, and he was sure he'd seen her somewhere before as she explained. "I raise chickens and keep a milk goat out back. As a widow woman, I have all the chores to do now."

"I'm sorry to hear that, ma'am. Is that how you got to be the coroner?"

"Of course. My late husband was elected to the job. Nobody wanted it when he died a couple of years ago, so the county let me carry on in his place. It's not as complicated a job as people think. Just take a little common sense."

He nodded soberly as he tried to remember where in hell he'd seen her before. She was one of those regular-featured gals, pretty but not distinctive enough to sort out from all the others worth a whistle. She was somewhere in her late thirties or early forties, give or take a hard life. He could see it didn't fluster her to be alone with a strange gent and wearing nothing but a dressing gown. She reached for a standard paper form and picked up her pen, saying, "Let's get it down on paper. I can fill in most of the blanks, seeing you're a known peace officer who got ambushed on the job. Just give me what happened in your own words."

Longarm filled her in, keeping to the facts the county really needed. She seemed surprised that the other prisoner had "escaped." She smiled wearily and asked, "Did he really get away clean or will I have to do this all again when they find him down the tracks at sunrise?"

He chuckled. "I really let him go. Don't put that down, though. I figured you had enough stale meat on your hands, even before I guessed your gender. Uh, do you have the body in the cellar or what, ma'am?"

She laughed. "Heavens, I'm the coroner, not the undertaker. The body's over at Moody's Funeral Parlour, if you want to see it."

"Don't have to. Already did. Listen, ma'am, I hope you won't take this as a forward question, but ain't we met somewhere before?"

She turned back to face him, with a sad little smile. "I was wondering if you'd remember me. Don't you ever forget a face, Longarm?"

He stared harder, shook his head, and said, "Nope. It was at the Alhambra, over to Dodge. I was riding for the Jingle Bob and you was—uh—serving drinks."

31

"I'll have you know that was *all* I served," she answered with a slight blush. "A girl has to live, and I never learned to rope and throw. I hope you don't have to mention my past to anyone in Trinidad, Longarm."

"I never gossip about old friends, Miss . . . Fanny, wasn't it?"

"I'm called Flora now. Flora Norris. My late husband, Peter Norris, didn't cotton much to Fanny, even though he was willing to make an honest woman of me."

Longarm nodded. "That sounds fair. But when we was both young and foolish back in Dodge, right after the War, I didn't go by the nickname of Longarm. How come you knew me that way, Flora?"

She smiled wistfully. "I've been following your career. I guess you know I had a sort of liking for you, back when we and the world were younger?"

"Do tell? You might have let *me* in on it! For I recall wasting a hell of a lot of drinking money in the Alhambra, feeling mighty lonesome after many a trail drive."

She turned away, her face a deeper shade of rose, and seemed flustered. "It was a long time ago, as you said. I'm a respectable widow woman and a county official now."

"I follow your drift. Where do you want me to sign for that rascal I had to gun?"

She slid the blank his way. He had to move closer to sign it. Her perfume was sure nice to inhale after breathing Trinidad air up to now. He was tempted to kiss her blushing cheek, but he just signed the paper and settled back in his bentwood chair. "I have to move on, ma'am," he said. "I was figuring on bedding down somewhere for the night. Somewhere a nosy, prowling rascal couldn't read my name off a register while I slept the sleep of the just. As a county official, you'd likely know of any handy no-questions establishments, right?"

"We don't have licensed parlor houses in this county, damn it. If you want to go across the tracks you'll find many a lady with a red lantern above her door. But you'll have to take your chances on how discreet and . . . healthy she might be."

He smiled sheepishly and said, "I wasn't looking for them kind of accommodations, Miss Flora. I've grown older and wiser since we were kids in Dodge. I'm really only looking for a safe place to bed down."

She thought for a moment. "Well, I guess I could put you up for the night," she said, then added quickly, "In the spare bedroom, of course. I know you don't believe me, but I really never served anything but drinks when you knew me at the Alhambra."

Longarm thought, too. Then he nodded and said, "Nobody saw me come in, so nobody's likely to come in after me. I'll pay for the night's lodgings, of course."

"That won't be needful, Longarm."

"Sure it will. I'm on an expense account and would have had to pay in any case. Why should you and your chickens be left out? How does a dollar a night sound to you?"

She laughed despite herself. "That's about right, for a room and nothing more," she said. "You'd know better than I what the going rate for other services might be."

She folded the death paper and put it in a drawer of her desk before rising to her feet. "All right, I'll show you to the spare room," she said.

Longarm got up, too, and placed a silver dollar on the desk before following her out.

Chapter 4

Flora led him down the hall to a guest room at the far end. The house was one story and, as it lay on a slope, the far end was dug into the side of the Front Range. So the windows were near the ceiling but still level with the grass outside. Longarm could see tassles of buffalo grass peeking over the moonlit sills at them before Flora lit the lamp on the bed table.

"The bath's next door," she said. "We have modern plumbing, but no hot water unless I build a fire under the water heater in the kitchen. Can it wait until morning?"

He said it could as he regarded the little room with approval. The bed was covered with a plump quilt and looked soft. It was more than wide enough for one, although two might have found it a mite snug. But Flora took care of that dawning notion by yawning and saying, "Well, as we've finished our business and you approve of the room, I'd better

34

say good night. I'm just down the hall, if you need anything."

He didn't know how to answer that, so he said nothing. She stepped out, shutting the door behind her. He shrugged, leaned the Winchester in a corner near the head of the bed, and hung up his hat and gunbelt. He drew the curtains across the windows, just in case, and sat on the bed. It felt as soft as it looked. He took his derringer and watch, chained together and more usually worn across the vest he'd left in Denver. He put the little .44 under a pillow, still chained to the watch. A man just never knew when he might want to know the time or fill his fist with a gun in the middle of the night. He started to unbutton his shirt, but decided not to yet. He didn't feel like sleeping and the night air was cold in the foothills even in high summer. He thought wistfully about the denim jacket rolled up with his other possibles and lashed to the borrowed stock saddle at the livery. He'd been dumb not to put it on after sunset. But he'd been so hot and stuffy riding down from Denver he'd just plain forgot to think ahead.

He took out the wire from Denver and read it, having nothing better to do. To his mild surprise, it contained some added information on the missing land-office gent. The land office was missing more than just Hiram Latimer.

Billy Vail had gotten Latimer's boss, Waterford, to go over the books when he got back to his office. Latimer had been out collecting range fees for six weeks or more, but he hadn't sent check one. As Billy Vail suggested in the wire, that could be taken a couple of ways. Latimer could have been killed before he collected any range fees, in which case a lot of cattlemen still owed Uncle Sam; or, Billy thought, someone might have killed him to rob his saddle-bags of the grazing money.

Longarm grimaced and decided he didn't like that notion much. He'd worked on more than one cattle spread in his day, and he'd been the ramrod at a couple. So he knew nobody paid land taxes or grazing fees in hard cash. If Latimer had been paid enough to matter, he'd been paid in checks made out to the government. Nobody but a fool would hold a man up for checks he couldn't cash. But, of course, nobody but a fool would have hired a pair of worthless drifters to gun the law.

He had some other data on Latimer in his saddlebags at the livery. He'd meant to read it, to pass the time on the long, tedious ride over lots of nothing much. He'd already scanned the little solid information Billy Vail had given him on the missing rascal. He couldn't come up with anything important to know tonight. He was still miles from where the land agent had last been seen alive.

He decided that turning in early made more sense than anything else he could come up with. But as he started unbuttoning again he felt itchy as hell, and he knew he'd mess Flora's sheets if he turned in needing a bath so bad. She'd said there was no hot water. She was likely in bed herself by now. He shrugged and let himself out to find the bathroom. It was as easy as she'd said. He lit the lamp and turned the hot water tap. The water was clean, but cold enough to give a polar bear goose bumps. *Think of it as a dive in a cool mountain stream on a hot and sticky day, old son,* he told himself.

It didn't help much. As he lowered his naked butt into the ice-cold water he supressed a gasp. But a man had to do what a man set out to do. He quickly lathered up with some stink-pretty soap he found, rinsed himself off even quicker and leaped out, trying not to curse out loud as he grabbed a towel to rub his goose bumps dry.

He shook out his shirt over the draining water, sat on the ice-cold seat of the commode, and hauled his grimy duds back aboard his now much cleaner body. He rinsed the tub clean, put out the lamp, and went back to his room. The house was quiet. Flora was either awake, or she didn't snore worth mention. He wondered if she wondered what on earth he'd been up to. It hadn't made much sense to him either.

He'd just sat down on his bed to strip some more when all hell busted loose outside. Longarm was on his feet grabbing for his gun rig as the last shots from somewhere nearby faded away in echoes. He headed down the hall as Flora popped her head out of her room to ask what happened.

He said, "Don't know. Mean to find out. Stay put and lock your door."

He got to the front door, fumbled the lock open, and stepped out on the porch just as a dark figure rounded the corner from the saloon, gun in hand and running in a crouch.

"Freeze!" Longarm snapped, as he threw down on the stranger, who didn't do as he was told at all. Longarm fired as the running man sent a bullet past him to thud into Flora's yellow clapboards. Longarm's aim was truer, and the stranger fired another round into the cinders ahead of him before flopping facedown in the rising black dust his last shot had stirred.

Longarm stayed put until he saw some figures rounding the corner, guns drawn. He called, "Everybody stop right there. I'm the law. I surely wish somebody would tell me what the hell's been going on around here!"

One of the town lawmen whom he'd met at the depot earlier spoke out. "Is that you, Longarm? That son of a bitch laying there just kilt a man cold-blooded in the Peacock around the corner!"

Longarm stepped down to join them. He holstered his .44. "This jasper had his gun in his left paw, too," he said. "One of you get his I.D., if any, while I confirm a suspicion about his victim."

He walked around the corner to the batwings of the saloon. Some of the men followed, and others examined the corpse he'd deposited in the street. Inside, the piano was no longer playing. Everyone was standing around something sprawled at their feet in one corner.

Longarm elbowed his way through and saw Jimbo lying there, as dead as he ever figured to get. "Damn it, kid," he muttered, "I told you to get out of town directly."

One of the town lawmen joined him, handing him a wallet as he stared down. "Hey, that looks like one of the owlhoots you caught up with at the depot earlier, Longarm," he said.

"I didn't catch up with them, exactly," Longarm said, "The left-handed son of a bitch outside sent *them* to catch up with *me*. This poor idjet made the mistake of looking him up for a payoff. He fibbed to me about not knowing old Lefty, or else he hoped Lefty would know him. That makes more sense. From the bullets in his shirt, I'd say Lefty caught him cold flat-footed."

As Longarm opened the wallet of the man he'd left to cool outside, one of the customers in the saloon spoke up. "I seen the whole thing. That dead kid, there, come in a few minutes ago, asking around if any of us knowed a gent calt Lefty who was said to drink here with a pal of his. None of us knowed any such gent, so nobody could help him. He got around to a moody-looking cowhand in black, sitting alone just over there, and when he asked the cowhand if he knowed anyone calt Lefty, the man just gunned him down like a dog and run out sort of wild-eyed."

Longarm nodded and said, "He looked sort of excited when we met up, too. According to this out-of-date voting card, his name was William Jones."

One of the town lawmen snorted. "Anyone could say he was a Jones, Longarm."

"Yeah. I didn't think he had much imagination. What I think we have here is a drifting no-good who hired out to do some heavy gunplay, lost his nerve, and tried to dupe a drinking buddy into taking the risk for around half his fee. Twelve hundred sounds more like my style."

He put the wallet away for now, turned to the helpful local law, and said, "Well, I'll go fill out some more fool papers with the lady coroner, if you boys will neaten up."

"No trouble, Longarm," said a man wearing a copper badge. "Yonder comes a couple of the undertaker's boys right now. You sure have been good for the undertaking business tonight, even if they all wind up in potter's field."

Longarm shook his head. "I want 'em all on ice and held in case anyone comes forward to claim 'em," he said.

"You think that's likely?"

"Nope. But it's worth a try. Up to now, the gang's been dumb as hell."

"Who do you think could be behind it all?" Flora Norris asked as she put the second batch of death papers away in her office.

Longarm shrugged. "I'm still working on that. I've been working for the Justice Department quite a few years since you last served me a beer. A man in my line collects enemies the way some collect stamps."

She said, "Tell me more about this mission you're on. It seems to me that someone may be mighty interested in it besides you and me."

He shook his head. "Already thought that notion out. Nobody here in Trinidad should have been expecting me. I didn't know I was on my way myself until earlier today. I just stopped off here to ride off to the east. Save for my office, who wired a message ahead for me, nobody back in Denver should have known I was Trinidad bound, either."

He thought for a moment, then added, "Now that's sort of spooky, when you really study on it. I know the rascals waiting for me at the depot had been recruited well in advance—and they had the right train, too."

He rose to his feet and yawned. "Well, since all three of 'em are on ice right now, it'd be a waste of time asking more details. I reckon I'll just have to sleep on it."

She followed him out and down the hall, repeating, "Tell me where you mean to ride, come sunrise. Sometimes two heads are better than one, and I've learned a thing or two about crime, holding down this job."

He entered his room. She did too. He sat down on the bed and said, "I ain't holding out on you 'cause I don't think a she-male public official ain't smart, Flora. I ain't fixing to tell you beans about what I may or may not be up to, because I'd hate to have a pretty gal on my suspicion list."

She sat down beside him on the bed, seemingly unaware

that her gown had opened at the top a mite. She gasped and said, "Surely you don't suspect *me* of anything!"

He smiled, enjoying the view even though he couldn't really see either of her nipples. "Of course I don't," he said. "I can't, since you don't know a thing about where I might be going or to do what. I mean to keep it that way, for your own good and my peace of mind. You see, honey, as a lawman pokes about, mulling things over in his head like an old cow chewing her cud, it helps if he don't have purely innocent names and faces distracting him."

"You mean, having forgotten me once, you mean to do it again?"

"In a way. Don't look injured, Flora. I never forgot you totally, even after all these years. A man never forgets a gal as handsome as you. But, at the risk of hurting your feelings, I'll confess I've never once thought of you in connection with any hunt I was on."

"Oh? How *did* you think of me then?"

"The way most men think of might-have-beens, alone and lonesome of an evening in a strange town."

She blushed and lowered her lashes. "Girls think of might-have-beens, too," she sighed. "We'd better change the subject. I'm really worried about that attempt on your life, Custis. Is it possible that someone knew you were on your way here because a confederate in Denver saw you getting on the southbound train?"

"Not hardly. I left early on a freight, lucky for me. But, hold on—you just gave me a grand notion! You're right about two heads being better than one, pard! I got to go out again. Don't wait up for me. Can't say how long I'll be. I'll see you over breakfast, Lord willing and the creeks don't rise."

He got up, put on his hat, and left as she was still asking him what on earth he meant to do at this hour. As she followed him to the front door, she said, "Wait—take this key. Everything decent will be closed now. You don't meant to visit any wicked gals across the tracks, do you?"

He laughed, said he'd have to study on that suggestion,

and left. He went first to the livery, tipped the night man another nickel, and got his denim jacket to put on. He felt warmer and the derringer and watch felt better, too, with their chain across his chest. He went to the Western Union office and greeted the same night clerk. "If a gent named Jones recieved a wire this afternoon, you'd have some record on it, right?" he asked.

The night man said he hadn't been on duty earlier, but he was willing to rummage. He leafed through a mess of blanks, and finally shook his head. "Not one wire from Denver to anyone here named Jones, Longarm," he said.

"All right. I didn't think it was his real name. How many wires from Denver came in, all told?"

"A score or more. Trinidad ships coal to Denver, and there's all sorts of business wires back and forth most every day."

"We can safely set *them* aside. The wire or wires I'm interested in would have been sent to someone *personal*, to be picked up here at the counter."

The Western Union man looked thoughtful. "Listen, we're sort of getting into deeper waters now," he said. "The company policy on personal messages is that they're personal. I can't let you read other folks' private wires, Longarm."

"Sure you can. I read good as hell. You can help by culling out any wires sent to folks you know to be solid citizens. I just want copies of any wire sent from Denver to be collected here under any name that don't ring a bell with you."

"Listen, I'm on your side, but I have my job to worry about, and company policy says—"

"Spare me the song and dance," Longarm cut in, adding, "I've had this discussion before, and I always win. Western Union has a lot of its wires strung across federal land, and I'm federal as hell. I could wire company headquarters. I could rustle up a local judge and get a court order. But, between you and me, it'd raise more suspicion of your common sense than it's worth to your retirement plans. So let's cut the bullshit, huh?"

The clerk started leafing through his copies, complaining about just aiming to do his job as he culled out a sheet here and there for Longarm. Longarm scanned them as they were handed across the counter. None of them read like an order to murder anyone. A couple were personal indeed, considering they'd been sent over open wires. He started stuffing them away. If any of the love notes, orders to buy or sell coal, or requesting money from home meant anything, they were in code. He'd have to study them all later. Nobody else from the Denver federal building had wired Trinidad. He hadn't expected anyone to. Only Billy Vail and Henry, his clerk, had seen Longarm's travel orders. He thanked the worried Western Union man and headed back to Flora Norris's house. He figured she'd be bedded down for the night by now. Her suggestion about the tenderloin across the tracks had been sort of interesting. He was feeling sort of horny now, for some fool reason, but he wasn't hard up enough to start paying for it. Besides, he meant to get an early start in the morning. No Man's Land was still a long ride off.

Chapter 5

The house was dark when Longarm got there. He let himself in and tiptoed down the hall carpet, not wanting to wake Flora up as he passed her door.

He groped his way to the guest room, decided not to bother striking a light, and hung up his hat, jacket, and gun rig before sitting on the bed to finish peeling. He leaped half out of his skin when he found the bed already occupied. Flora saved herself a punch in the mouth by whispering, "It's me. Did I startle you?"

He relaxed a little. "You surely did," he said. "*Surprised* the hell out of me, too!"

"Didn't you expect to find me here, Custis?"

He hadn't, but as he started shucking he didn't have to ask why. He'd spent a lot of time at the old Alhambra in Dodge, and she'd already said that gals had such memories and regrets, too.

So he rolled under the covers with Flora, naked, to find that she was in the same condition, and a mighty friendly position. As he mounted her like an old lover coming home, she wrapped her arms and legs around him and gasped "Oh, yes!" as he entered her.

He did some pleasant gasping, too, for whether it was true or not that she'd only served drinks at the Alhambra, her past and widowhood lay far enough back for her to be tight and hungry between her soft thighs. She'd had a head start on him by lying there so long feeling horny, so she climaxed almost at once, pleaded for mercy as he kept pounding hard, and then clenched her teeth and groaned. "Oh, Jesus, it's even better than I imagined it would be," she murmured. "I knew you were a big man, but this is almost too much for me."

"Am I hurting you?" he asked, slowing to a gentle gallop in her love saddle.

She hugged him tighter. "Yes, but I love it. Do it harder, faster—I think I'm about to... Oh, God, I am!"

He came right after her, her contractions inspiring him to new heights.

She chuckled fondly. "I felt that. I know you never went across the tracks tonight after all. Oh, Custis, I was so afraid this wouldn't happen. How did you know I wanted you?"

That was a mighty silly question coming from a lady he'd found naked in his bed, but he answered politely, "I told you I'd often thought about the chances we passed up in Dodge when we were younger and more shy."

She thrust her hips up to take him deeper. "Oh, to think of all those wasted opportunities." Then she laughed. "I was a virgin then. This probably would have killed me. My God, it seems to be getting even bigger! How did you ever learn to do that, Custis?"

"I never. The fool thing has a mind of its own, and now that we've sort of busted the ice..."

"Oh, my, it's like losing my cherry all over again! Am I doing it right for you, darling? I'm not really as experienced as you, despite the way we met."

"You're doing fine for a semi-virgin," he lied, gently. Some gals were just like that, getting to know a gent in the Biblical sense. She'd up and said she'd been married at least once, and she was screwing him back like an expensive whore showing off to a pal on her night off. But he knew she wanted to be thought of as a lady—sort of—so he resisted the impulse to throw back his head and yell "Powder River and let her buck!" as he ejaculated in her without further comment.

He figured he had one more round in his magazine this side of a rest and a smoke. But he'd been wrong about the night air being cold in the foothills at night, it seemed. He threw off the covers, withdrew long enought to roll her over on her hands and knees, and got back in her dog-style, to do it hotter but less sweaty. Flora gasped that she'd never done it in such an undignified position before, but then she arched her spine to take it to the roots as she chewed on the corner of a pillow, growling deep in her throat like a she-male mountain lion in heat. He grabbed a hip bone in each hand and pulled her on and off like a tight little boot filled with whipped cream. She beat him coming that way, too, and they wound up side ways in a mighty tangled position as he exploded in her pulsing flesh.

When they came up for air, she kissed him and purred, "You're just awful. And, honest to God, I have to stop being Fanny and get Flora back. You're driving me out of my mind!"

That sounded fair. So he disengaged, pulled the covers back over them, and fumbled for a smoke from his shirt on the end table as she snuggled against him, nuzzling his collarbone softly and making little puppy noises. He held the cheroot in his teeth, found a match, and thumbed a light. Flora looked up at him adoringly in the flickering glow as he lit his smoke. "God, you're good looking," she said.

The soft light was kind to her, too, so he said so before he shook the match out, took the smoke from his mouth, and kissed her. As they snuggled down more comfortably, she said, "No, I really mean it. I guess you were a little younger than me in the first place, when we met in Dodge. Time's cruel teeth are much harder on a woman, Custis. Do you find me a silly old woman, now?"

"Old? Hell, girl, you're just starting to lose your baby fat. I admire a gal with a little character in her face."

"Wrinkles, you mean. I'm glad the lamp is out. I'm ashamed of the way my breasts sag now."

He held the cheroot in his teeth to fondle those breasts with a free hand as he said judiciously, "You still got nice tits, Flora. The trouble with you is that you're a perfectionist, like most women. The only reason men seem to age more graceful is that we don't fret as much about a line or two here and there. I hear German dudes pay money to have fake dueling scars put on to make 'em look distinguished. Gals are afraid a few laugh lines or mayhaps an old bullet hole makes 'em unfit for further human consumption. I like you just fine the way you are. Your skin feels soft as silk all over—and, hell, I'm way more scuffed up than you."

She sighed. "You're right. A woman as weather-beaten as you *would* be considered old and ugly. You just keep looking better every time I see you. But I'm still mighty grateful for the dark."

He let it go for now as he enjoyed the smoke and her body nestled soft and sweet-smelling against him. He'd gotten his wind back and the cheroot was about done when he could tell, from the way her hand had shyly wandered, that she was getting impatient.

He rolled half atop her to snuff out the cheroot. Then he struck another match and lit the lamp by the bed. She gasped, "What are you doing?" and hunkered down under the quilts.

He said, "I'm trying to prove a point. You have to get over this shy streak, Flora. I'd have done this to you years ago if you hadn't always looked at me so coy. You got to get used to the notion that you and your body are beautiful, and will be for a good twenty years or more."

As he started to throw the covers down she protested. "No! Not with the lamp lit! I'm too embarrassed!"

46

But he remounted her, kissing her to keep her quiet as he entered her again and started moving. Her tongue darted into his mouth as she started moving in rhythm with his long, firm strokes. When he had her really going he took his lips from her and stiff-armed himself above her, smiling down. "A man likes to see what he's getting into, and all I see is nice as hell!" he said. "Look down between us, Flora. Look down and see it parting that pretty strawberry bush!"

She gasped, red-faced. "Oh, you're just awful!" she said. But then she suddenly did as she was told, and gasped again. "My God, I can see myself getting . . . you know!"

"'Fucked' is the word you're groping for, honey. It ain't a bad word as used between friends. Ain't you ever fucked with the lights on before?"

"No, and it seems terribly wicked! Why do you talk dirty to me, Custis? Haven't I been—well—fucking you right?"

Then she blushed beet-red and covered her face with her hands as he started pounding harder. But as she began to climax, too, she peeked down through her fingers and gasped, "Oh, I'm coming, and I can see what you're doing to make me come, and it's . . . it's beautiful!"

After that Flora was ready for some real old country loving and by the time they'd done it once more, with the lamp lit, she confessed that she just couldn't understand why she'd ever been so bashful.

He kissed her nipples as she cupped her breasts to him—her on top, of course—and in the end he seemed to have convinced her he thought her tits were mighty pretty. They both wanted to keep going but, being only human, they finally had to stop, trim the lamp, and fall asleep in each other's arms.

When he next woke up, on top of her again and moving fine for a man who'd thought he was just dreaming about it, it was daylight. So it was a good thing she'd gotten over her shyness. They screwed themselves awake, went arm-in-arm to the kitchen, naked, and he had her again on the kitchen table as they waited for the wood range to heat up.

It was a hell of a way to work up an appetite for ham and eggs.

They broke fast smiling at one another across the table, both naked as jays. She said if anyone came to her door she didn't mean to answer—not until she came some more, herself. She asked Longarm how long he could stay. He regarded her soberly and said, "I should have been on my way by now. I got some serious riding ahead, honey."

She started to cry. She wiped her face with her hand and said, "I'm sorry, darling. I knew last night would be all there was. Forgive me. It's just that it took us so long to get friendly and it's over so soon."

"I might be coming back this way, once my job's done," he said. It was a lie and they both knew it. "You'll always find the same welcome, you brute," she said. "Is there time—you know—to say goodbye properly?"

He knew there wasn't, not if he paid attention to orders, at any rate. On the other hand, he'd saved his own life the night before by bending the rules about train connections. "If I stayed the day or more, it'd still hurt as much in the end, Flora," he replied.

She looked up like a drowning woman spotting a straw and pleaded, "Just one more day, darling? I could put the shades down and leave the 'closed' sign at the front door. Hardly anyone ever comes here on business when men like you aren't in town, and I need a man like you more than I thought I did. It's been so long, and I'm so love-starved!"

He sighed. "Oh, hell, I can make up the lost time by trotting my ponies a few extra hours. But can I have some more coffee first? I can see a man has to stay awake if he means to keep *you* company in bed!"

Farther east, where the foothills began to give way to the rolling prairie of the High Plains, a hogback ridge of red sandstone rose above the wagon trace leading out of Trinidad. As the sun rose higher, a big prairie grasshopper buzzed like a rattlesnake as the warming sun woke it up. One of the two men lying in wait atop the hogback flinched

48

at the sound. His partner laughed and said, "It's a grass-hopper, pard. We're too high in the sky for the real thing. Hardly any prairie rattlers at this altitude."

The man who'd flinched shifted the rifle across his el-bows. "I knowed what it was, damn it," he said. "I just don't cotton to sudden noises. What time is it?"

"Going on nine. Simmer down, He'll be along directly. Longarm tolt 'em in town he'd be riding out at sunrise, and any fool can see the sun has riz."

"I don't like it. That big bastard's slicker than a greased pig, and they tolt Matt and Jimbo he'd be on the train from Denver, too."

"Shit, them idjets wasn't pros, like us. I don't know how Longarm got the drop on them and Lefty last night. But, as any fool can see, he ain't about to do the same to *us!* We're forted good on the only high ground for a country mile. Look around you. You see anything but summer-kilt short grass in ever' direction? How in thunder would even Longarm be able to pussyfoot up ahint us here?"

The worried one looked around, shrugged, and said, "He don't have to get the drop on us. He only has to go *around.* And I fear that's what the son of a bitch just did."

"Simmer down. This is the trail to No Man's Land from Trinidad, ain't it?"

"It is, but that grass you're so fond of stretches over the horizon in ever' direction. There's no law saying Longarm had to follow that wagon trace down there. What if he just cut across country? He'd have passed this rock by now if he'd taken the regular trail out at dawn."

His partner patted the action of his Henry Rifle. "He ain't ever going to pass this rock," he replied. "That's why the boss tolt us to wait for him here. Don't worry, he'll be along any minute. I've worked longer hours for a lot less pay in my time."

"Yeah, they made me bust rocks when I was in the state prison, too. But it's getting late, damn it! How long do you have to fry atop this rock afore you can see he must have took another route?"

The man with the Henry frowned. "We'll give him till noon," he decided. "The boss can be surly about excuses, but he ought to buy your notion of another route if we hold out until it's plain impossible that Longarm took the trail the boss expected."

Back at Flora's, Longarm of course had no way of knowing how fortunate it was that he was neglecting his duty to the rest of the taxpaying public. Flora paid taxes, and she surely liked to carry on scandalous for a gal who said she'd never done it without a nightgown on before. She took a notion to have them "Haunt," as she put it, every stick of soft furniture in her house as she led him, laughing, from room to room in his birthday suit. She got the idea while they were doing it in her own bigger bed for a change. She said her bed wouldn't feel as lonesome as she waited for him, now that they'd "haunted" it. She took him into the parlor and they did it on the sofa, so the sofa wouldn't feel jealous of the two beds and the kitchen table. It was even more fun doing it to her in the matching armchair, with one of Flora's knees hooked over either arm. But when she suggested doing it on the rosewood coffee table he said it sounded silly and asked if there wasn't some more cushioned stuff.

They had cake and coffee to get their wind back. Then she took him to her office. Her swivel chair was fun. Longarm sat in it while Flora put a knee over each of the chair's arms, too, and they swiveled until she came. Longarm was still hot when she levered herself off, climbed up on her rolltop desk, and reclined against the cubbyholes of dry, dull papers with her thighs spread invitingly. Longarm pondered, opened two drawers for her to brace her bare heels in, and had her that way, standing up.

They haunted the hall rug while they waited for the water tank to heat up. Then they took a hot bath together. She'd adjusted the mirror so she could watch herself being just awful as she got on top in the tub, slithery with suds and splashing half the water on the floor.

They finally wound up back where they'd started, in the

guest room bed. Longarm was feeling mighty ashamed of himself by now. Not for doing it so many ways in front of mirrors and such, but because the day was damned near shot. He'd been naughty in a way Billy Vail never would approve, and hell, anything got to be *work,* once you'd been at it long enough.

Flora almost dozed in his arms, murmuring that he was the most virile man she'd ever met. He took it as a real compliment, for, despite her shy ways, no woman could ever have learned to do it so well with only one husband to practice on.

He didn't answer. He didn't smoke, and, as he'd hoped, Flora fell sound asleep beside him. It was tempting as hell to join her, but it was well past high noon, and if they woke up together, he'd not only have to face a tearsome goodbye, but likely some more acrobatics.

He felt sated as a kid who'd been locked for the night in a candy store right now. He knew he might not if he got some rest and woke up with anything this nice playing with his fool organ grinder. So he waited until she rolled onto her face, breathing gently, and as gently worked his way off the edge of the bed without disturbing her. He scooped up his things, carried them out to the kitchen, and sat down to dress as he smiled at the bare table, remembering how much nicer it had looked with Flora spread across it naked, rolling her strawberry blonde head from side to side as he stood there thrusting into her strawberry bush. There was still some coffee on the range. It was cold, but he inhaled a cup of it anyway. Then he put the key she'd given him on the table and let himself out, locking the spring catch after him.

He was in her backyard. He didn't see any chicken coop or goat shed. He chuckled and let himself out the garden gate. The poor old gal had been undressed early because she'd been expecting him. The local law had told their coroner he'd be coming and, knowing who he was, Flora had been plotting against his virtue from the start.

There was nobody in sight until he reached the main

51

street, strode down to the livery, and got his ponies. He rode out of Trinidad around two in the afternoon, feeling guilty. Nothing happened when he passed the big red sandstone hogback. He didn't know he'd just proven, once again, that virtue wasn't always its own reward.

Chapter 6

It took Longarm close to three days to recover from Flora Norris and make it to the west end of the No Man's Land strip, where Latimer had last been seen alive. He camped with his borrowed ponies on the lone prairie, changing mounts from time to time to keep the cow ponies as frisky as when he'd borrowed them from the Diamond K. One was a bay gelding called Browny and the other a pinto mare called Paint. The boys at the Diamond K had too big a remuda to bother with original names.

He passed spreads and homesteads as he worked his way east, of course, but he swung wide to avoid human contact. He wasn't feeling surly. He knew that anyone passing a lonesome settler was supposed to be polite and spend an hour or so jawing with the folk. He was in too big a hurry to serve as a newspaper or entertainer, and some old hermits could get proddy as hell if you refused a friendly invite to stay and have some coffee.

He made up the wasted half-day at Flora's along the way, and as his glands recovered he wasn't sure it had really been wasted. When he awoke one morning with a hard-on he knew he'd been cured, but the only she-male for miles around was Paint, and he wasn't *that* desperate.

He discussed the matter with each pony in turn as he rode them. They offered no explanations as to why human feelings were so spiteful, either. Being horses, and one of them sexless, they likely didn't know how dumb it was to pine for a strawberry blonde a day or so after he could have sworn on the Good Book he never wanted to kiss her again.

As they trended away from the Rockies, the land kept getting lower and drier. The High Plains sloped gently from the lap of the high backbone of the continent all the way to the bottom lands of the sluggish brown Missouri–Mississippi. It took about eight hundred miles, so the slope wasn't really noticeable.

He started passing clumps of chaparral that shouldn't have been this far north. It was no mystery, though. Despite the fact that the spreads he'd passed were too far apart to see any two low roof tops at the same time, the short grass all around was shamefully overgrazed. From time to time he'd pass a longhorn or two. The critters knew it was getting on to roundup time, and mostly spooked and ran off when they spotted him. To an Eastern eye, the range would have seemed thinly populated by livestock. Back East, where it rained more, a whole dairy herd could manage on a forty-acre meadow, given supplemental feeding and handy water. Out here it took a dozen acres or more to feed one cow. As most of the folk had started out back East, a lot of them didn't savvy that. It took a lot of slow-growing, summer-killed shortgrass to keep even a tough old longhorn going. The range around him showed there were just too many, widespread as they might seem.

The brush got worse as they approached the supposedly unclaimed land of the overlooked strip. Longarm had scorned the chaps some of the Rocking X hands had been wearing, and he'd wondered why an experienced range fee man like Latimer had shown up at the Denver office wearing chaps—until now.

He hadn't thought to borrow any chaps. The last time he'd been down this way the shortgrass had been taller and there'd been no brush worth mention. Now, in places the chaparral was so thick he had to ride around. In others, the prairie grew the way it was supposed to for a few miles. As he rode toward more brush in the distance he figured out why the land was a checkerboard of brush and open grass. A small herd of longhorn burst out of the brush and lit out to the north in a cloud of dust. Longarm stood tall in his stirrups and, sure enough, just over the horizon he could make out the spinning vanes of a sunflower windmill.

Cows needed more than dry grass or whatever the hell they found in chaparral to nibble. Cows needed water, lots of water, when forced to forage sun-baked straw. So you seldom saw cows more than a few hours' walk, cow style, from a water hole.

Local cattlemen had built tanks fed by windmills here and there across the open plain. So the results were overgrazing near the windmills and plenty of shortgrass but no cows where a cow wasn't up to walking in less than half a day. At this time of the year, there were no natural water holes or running streams on the High Plains. The soil was deep. Bedrock was way the hell down, and such summer rain as there might be soaked into the earth as if it were a thirsty sponge.

Just thinking about this made Longarm thirsty. He'd noticed that his water bags, packed by the pony he wasn't riding, were sort of low. He took out his survey map and unfolded it as he told Paint, "All right, we'd best detour over there and refill our water bags, old gal. You just move along while I figure out where the hell we may be."

Navigating on the High Plains was a lot like navigating on the sea. Like an old salt, a plainsman could find his way where a tenderfoot would get lost without obvious landmarks to guide him. Aside from dead reckoning by watch and compass, Longarm had a feel for the lay of the land after all the times he'd gotten turned around out here, learning. A glance at the grass stems gave an educated guess about prevailing winds, which tended to come from the west when the sky wasn't doing anything exciting. High clouds told the same story, and anyone with a watch and the sun to look at hardly ever had to fish a compass out of his saddlebag. Longarm told Paint, "We're just inside the northwest corner of the strip. Yon windmill's got to be on the Colorado side of the line, if they don't want to be arrested. If old Latimer ever passed this way, he'd have wanted to talk to them about the way their damned cows are ruining Uncle Sam's range. So *we'd* best talk to them, too."

It took longer than some might have expected to reach the windmill. Longarm was used to the way the clear air made things seem closer out here, so he wasn't surprised that it took forever before they topped a rise and saw the spread the windmill was watering.

It looked as though it could have used more water. There were no trees, and where some might have planted a garden there was only bare, dry dirt with a shabby sod house and some sun-bleached pole corrals to show for what must have been a lot of work in the beginning.

The windmill was the prettiest thing on the spread. It stood fifty yards from the house. Its galvanized iron blades sparkled as they turned against the cobalt-blue sky. A rusty pipe from the pump at the base of the windmill derrick ran another hundred yards out to a corrugated iron tank surrounded by some of the cows Longarm had spooked earlier.

There was no water line to the house. People who raised cows hardscrabble expected their women and kids to carry the water in as needed. Watering the stock was more important. A man with land could always get a woman, and kids came naturally. It was a lot harder to build a decent herd.

As he rode Paint down the slope, leading Browny, a barefoot kid wearing bib overalls and nothing else came out of the house with a shotgun. The kid's hair was dull brown and hung down to the shoulders, so Longarm wasn't sure if it was a he or a she. The kid was so ugly it hardly mattered.

Longarm studied on how to address the youngster as he rode within hailing range. It could be a mortal mistake to call a boy who was holding a gun on him a gal. On the other hand, an ugly little gal was just as likely to get surly if you called her a boy. Longarm decided just to call it "kid" for now. There was no denying *that* part.

He reined in and called out, "Howdy, kid. My handle is Custis Long, and my ponies and me need water and a few directions."

The kid said, "You can't come in the house. Pa and the boys is out riding the range, and Pa said to shoot any varmints as come on our claim."

"Well, that sounds sensible. But I ain't a varmint, I'm a U. S. federal agent, so if you shot me, your Pa would likely give you a good tanning."

The kid frowned and thought. Longarm could see thinking was an effort he or she wasn't used to. Finally it said, "Well, you can fill your water bags at yonder tank, but don't try anything *tricky,* for I've got you covered."

"I swear I won't put any of them cows in my saddlebag. Do you have a name, kid?"

"I do. It's Shirly Ann, and Pa says if any man trifles with me I'm to blow his balls off with this scattergun, so don't get horny, hear?"

"I just want to get some water," said Longarm soberly, neck-reining Paint toward the water tank. It made the hairs on the back of his neck tingle to face away from the ugly little gal as she followed on foot with that shotgun. But folks who really meant to gun a man seldom harped about the possibility. She likely wouldn't shoot unless he made some sudden move that confused her weak mind. So, as the cows around the water tank poked off, lowing unhappily, Longarm waited until both ponies were lined up drinking from the tank, then told the kid, "I'm aiming to dismount now, and you can see my saddle gun's in its boot and my hands ain't anywhere near my side arm, Miss Shirly Ann."

She said, "Well, all right, but don't try anything *funny,* hear?"

He dismounted, moved casually around to the pack saddle on Browny, and unfastened the water bags. He dumped the meager contents on the ground, since such water as was left was warm and stagnant. It would have been good for the grass, if any grass had been able to grow within the limits of the hardscrabble spread. At least the water laid the dust some. He started refilling the bags from the corrugated iron tank as he asked casually, "Can I take it we'd be just north of the No Man's Land line, Miss Shirly Ann?"

"Sure. That's where Pa and the boys rid off, searching for market beef. As anyone can see, some few cows still don't know roundup time's coming. But most of the herd is skulking out in the infernal brush."

"I've noticed how reluctant longhorns are to become beefsteak. If you carried some white faces here, they'd be easier to herd and worth more as beef."

"Pa knows that. Did you take us for ignorant folk? You're dressed like a cowboy. How come you don't know more about cows? Shoot, I'm fourteen, and I can tell you why we still graze longhorn. Ain't another brute as could *graze* on such worthless range."

Longarm took one heavy water bag and set it aside as he started to fill the other. "I noticed the land all about has been overgrazed mighty bad, Miss Shirly. Wouldn't it make more sense to keep a smaller, better herd of high-grade critters?"

She shrugged and lowered the shotgun muzzle, either to be polite or, more likely, because it was getting too heavy for her skinny arms. She said, "Takes money to buy high-grade beef, and money's hard to come by when you only have low-grade scrub longhorns to sell. As to overgrazing, as Pa always says, it ain't our grass, so why should we worry if it's overgrazed or not?"

"I admire his forethought," said Longarm dryly. "I'm

sure glad it's this year and not next. For, any minute now, this part of the world figures to blow clean away. Seeing as you brought the matter up, it was my understanding you stock raisers strung along this line had to *pay* for the government grass your cows ate."

She said, "Already did, this year. That's why we got a right to *all* of it, down to the roots! Another government man come by just a short time ago. Pa paid him for our range permit."

"Do tell? Was the gent's name Latimer? Hiram Latimer?"

"It was. He comes by regular. Him and Pa had an awesome row about how many cows we had. That sneaky federal man rode our range some afore he rode in to collect. He said he'd tallied our herd and come close to calling Pa a liar when Pa said he didn't have half that many cows."

"Well, folks collecting for the government are like that. I don't suppose I could see your range permit, Miss Shirly Ann?"

"Range permit? I just told you we had one, dang it."

"Yeah, but you're supposed to have it down on paper. Is it in the house? Does your dad carry it on him, or what?"

She frowned. "I disremember Mr. Latimer *giving* Pa anything. Pa wrote him a check and Latimer put it in his saddlebag. Pa keeps old canceled checks in his desk. You can't see 'em. I dasn't let you in the house with the menfolk gone, lest you throw me down and rob me of my virtue."

Longarm nearly gagged at the thought. He'd awoken with an erection at dawn, but a man had to draw the line. He said, "Well, if your Pa pays by check, he likely don't need a receipt. I'm not boned up on the way the land office does business. I'm a lawman, not a bill collector."

The ugly young girl replied, "Someone sure must have *done* something in these parts. You're the third lawman who's rid by in the last day or so."

"Do tell? I didn't know any other lawmen were working on this case. Did they say who they were, and who they might be looking for?"

"They didn't give their names. Not to me, leastways. They talked to Pa yesterday. He said later that they was tracking a lone rider who'd got past them, leaving Trinidad. They descripted him to Pa, but Pa couldn't help, since you're the first lone rider as has rid past in over a week or more."

Her eyes suddenly narrowed thoughtfully. Then she shrugged. "Nope, *that* won't work. You come *after*. They couldn't be tracking *you*."

"I can see you're right smart, for a pretty young gal. Can I take it that if I head due east, I'll find other outfits strung along the unmarked border like crow birds on a telegraph line?"

"Sure. Everybody builds their windmill as close to the free range as they can put her. The next spread's about six or eight miles, and you can see their sunflower from high ground. I would ride around the Tumbling H if I was you, though. The owner's loco."

"How so, loco, Miss Shirly Ann?"

"Just loco loco. I never met up with 'em. Pa says to stay away from 'em. He had trouble with 'em right after we got here a few years back. Went over to be neighborly and come home with birdshot in his hide. The boys wanted to ride over and settle up, but Pa said to let it be. Said we was here to raise cows, not to have a war."

"I can see your Pa's a sensible man and, hell, you'll doubtless be full grown and moved away before this whole range blows away in dust. So I thank you for the water and the information, and as soon as I shift saddles we'll be on our way."

He started to do so. It was Browny's turn to carry him. As he uncinched the stock saddle, Shirly Ann asked, "Do you really think I'm pretty?"

"I said so, didn't I?"

"You did. I was just thinking. Pa and the boys will likely be out on the range all day. So if I was to invite you inside for a spell, who'd ever *know* about it?"

"We would, Miss Shirly Ann. Your offer's mighty tempting, but . . ."

"I'll confess I'm tempted, too. You're sort of pretty, and — well — I sure do like to screw."

Longarm hauled the saddle off and laid it aside to uncinch the pack saddle aboard Browny as he said conversationally, "That's sort of bold talk, coming from a fourteen-year-old virgin gal, ma'am."

"Don't you want to screw me? Pa says I screw good as hell for a virgin. The boys do, too. My brother Tom says I'm better than any of the fancy gals in town."

"I'm sure he'd know. I thank you for the invite from the bottom of my heart. But maybe another time, Miss Shirly Ann. I have a long ways to ride while the sun ball still stands high to light my way."

He resaddled faster than he'd meant to, starting out. For folks who called their neighbors loco, these folks were mighty carefree. It was a good thing incest wasn't a federal crime. He knew better than to tell her what the State of Colorado would do to her menfolk if she ever had this same conversation with a local badge.

As he mounted up, water bags refilled and a fresh pony under him, the ugly little gal called out, "Look!" So he did.

Shirly Ann had leaned the shotgun against the water tank and dropped her bib overalls around her ankles.

As she stood there, jaybird naked, he tried to think of a time he'd seen a more awful sight, but he nodded politely. "You sure have a nice build, Miss Shirly Ann. But, like I said, I'm in a hurry."

He swung Browny around and rode off fast, leading Paint, to get out of range before she went even crazier. She called after him that he was a mean-hearted, hateful man who likely preferred boys. He didn't look back. He didn't have to. The vision of that skinny, naked body would haunt him for a spell.

Chapter 7

Longarm headed back up the rise he'd come down from, trending east at an angle. When it was safe to rein in and look around, he could see a dot on the eastern skyline that seemed to be spinning in the wind. He heeled his mount forward, bearing on the distant windmill. Navigating along the north line of the strip was going to be easier than expected, with open rangers strung along so close to what they thought of as free grass.

But it *wasn't* free grass, damn it! The despoiled range to his right belonged to the government, and at the rate these hardscrabble outfits were going, it would soon be a dusty desert.

He didn't remember how much a head the Land Management folks charged, but it had to be set too low. Some fool back in Washington who'd never seen the dry High Plains doubtless set the standards based on some Maryland dairy farm's capacity to carry cows. Low rates for unfenced open range had attracted idjets who aimed to gut and git. Since it wasn't their own land they were ruining, it would be a waste of time to lecture them on proper range management. The price of beef was up, back East. So the West was shipping it now, and to hell with the future.

The crazy little gal back there had been wrong about the distance to the Tumbling H. Ponies trotted about six miles an hour. It took more like three to get close enough to matter. He'd walked his ponies part of the way, but he still made it over twelve miles. As he got closer to the windmill he saw that the kid back there had made a natural mistake. Things not only looked closer on the High Plains, but the windmill was enormous. It stood head and shoulders over most of the windmills he'd ever seen. He reined in on a rise and studied the layout ahead, remembering that the kid said the folks here were loco—by her standards.

The windmill was set up a good distance from the house and outbuildings and fed a stock tank big enough to go swimming in. They'd planted a good-sized kitchen garden, neatly fenced in with white pickets. The sod house and outbuildings had been whitewashed, too. More wondrous yet, grass grew almost to the dooryard. It was welcome-mat short and summer-killed, but at least the Tumbling H didn't let its stock graze roots. He looked south and saw that while there was far too much brush to call the range well managed, there were swards of open grass here and about. He saw a couple of horses regarding him suspiciously from a distance. There were some more horses in the corral behind the house ahead. He nodded and told his own mount, "It's a horse-breeding outfit. That's why there's still some grass about. You creatures pine away on nothing but rough grazing, so the Tumbling H feeds extra grain. That silo next to the barn is likely filled with cracked corn, or even oats. Looks like a prosperous spread for these parts."

He rode on, leading Paint. As they got closer, he heard singing. A high-pitched voice was singing, "Oh, the last time I seen her, and I ain't seen her since, she was trying to fuck a nigger, through a bobwire fence!"

The song broke off sudden and Longarm knew he'd been spotted. He rode up to the house, dismounted, and proceeded to tether his brutes to the hitching rail in the dooryard. The door would open, and someone would say if he was welcome or should ride on.

But nothing happened. He stood there in the hot sun, staring at the curtained windows on either side of the plank door. The curtains were too thick to see through and nobody inside was moving them to peek. He shrugged, walked up to the door, and knocked politely.

Still nothing. He frowned, wondering what he ought to do about this odd reception. He knew someone was about. Windmills didn't sing dirty songs, no matter how the wind might blow.

He sat on the doorstep, took out a cheroot, and lit up. Mayhaps the gal who'd been singing was alone and shy. Sooner or later someone wearing pants would ride back in. A spread this size figured to carry at least two hired hands and, what the hell, he and his ponies were both in need of a break, so he could wait a spell.

He waited maybe ten minutes, wishing they'd thought to build a proper veranda with some shade, and then a distant she-male voice called out, "Hey, stranger?"

He looked toward the sound to see a head peering over the rim of the big water tank at him from about a hundred yards or more. He stood up and started walking that way. The gal in the water tank yelled, "Don't come no closer! I got no duds on!"

Longarm stopped and called back, "I can see I caught you singing in the bath, ma'am. I don't mean to come no closer. But how do you reckon we ought to work this out?"

"You could ride on, damn it. I wasn't expecting company!"

He nodded. "I figured as much. It's your property and so it's your say. I'm sorry I upset you and I'll just be on my way. But could you tell me how far the next spread east might be?"

"Ten, twelve miles. Who did you say you was?"

"Name's Custis Long, ma'am. I ride for Uncle Sam. But as I can see you ain't receiving this afternoon, I'll just mount up and we'll say no more about it."

He walked over the the hitching rail. She called out, "Wait up. Let's study on this. I ain't an inhospitable woman, but I ain't got a stitch on, neither, and my duds are in the house behind you."

"You walked all the way over there naked, in broad day?"

"How was I to know anyone would drop by? There's not supposed to be another soul within miles. I'll tell you what. You just go inside and fetch me my dress. You'll find it draped over a chair just inside the door. The door ain't locked."

Longarm nodded, went back to the house, and turned the latch. Inside, he noticed that the sod walls had been papered. The wallpaper was only newspaper, but it doubtless kept the dust from falling off the walls during dry spells. A blue and white print dress was draped over a bentwood chair, as she'd said. He picked it up, noting that it was about the right size for a woman built nicely. He folded it over his arm and went out again. As he strode toward the water tank, the gal staring back at him over the rim turned out to be a well tanned brunette with big, wide-set eyes which matched the sky above. As he got closer, she said, "Circle around to the far side from the house."

He said her plan made sense as he moved to obey. She circled the tank with him, keeping her invisible charms against the corrugated iron sides as she said, "Howdy. I'm Betty Harris. Some call me the Spooky Widow Harris. But I don't figure I'm spooky, do you?"

"No, ma'am. The little I can see of you looks sensible enough. I reckon I'd cool off in that tank on a day like this if it was mine and the nearest neighbors were over the horizon, too."

She dimpled. "I can see you're a live-and-let-live gent. But I ain't getting out in front of you, anyway. Lay the dress there in the grass. Then—let's see—if you was to go back towards the house, with your back turned to me . . ."

65

"I think that'd work, too." He nodded, spreading her print dress on the grass behind the tank.

As he turned away, she went on, "Go on in the house and I'll join you in a minute, hear?"

He did as he was told, walking fast. But when he got inside and peered out the window between the drapes he could see that she'd rolled her naked form over the far side already, damn it. As he watched, she came around the tank, barefoot and looking soggy in her ankle-length cotton dress. He moved from the window and sat down at the table in the middle of the two-room soddy. There was an ashtray, so he used it. He noticed a cigar butt someone else had left earlier. He'd been right about hired hands, it would seem. But they couldn't be riding close, unless she was a mighty free thinker indeed.

The woman came in, smelling wet and clean. She said, "I reckon the air's dry enough to risk an ague in this wet dress. It sure feels cooler now than when I yielded to temptation earlier this afternoon. You just set a spell whilst I coffee and cake you. If you're really hungry, I could rustle up some ham and eggs. Eggs are pickled in water glass, but they ain't bad."

Longarm shook his head. "Coffee and cake sounds fine, ma'am. But if you have some oats to spare, I'd surely like to buy some off you before we leave. My ponies have been eating more than I figured cow ponies might."

"I got plenty of oats, and I don't charge for 'em. You say you're a federal man? I just paid one of you boys for a year's grazing, a few weeks back."

"Was his name Latimer, and could you date it more exact, ma'am?"

She moved over by her wood range and opened a cupboard with her back to Longarm. "He was Hiram Latimer, all right. Can't say the exact date, for one day's much the same as any other on this infernal lonely spread."

He stared down at the cigar butt and muttered, "Yeah, prairie life is hard on she-males, with the menfolk gone most of the time."

She turned with a sigh and half a sponge cake on a tray as she said, "I have no menfolk hereabouts, now. My man was killed a year ago come frost. I've been carrying on alone, and I don't mind telling you it ain't been easy, Custis Long."

"I'd say it was impossible. Do you smoke cigars, Miss Betty?"

"Sure do. I've never learned to roll a cigarette, and dipping snuff is disgusting. As to how I manage alone out here, my late husband and me had about proved out our claim when he was bushwhacked. I reckon the bastards figured I'd pull up stakes and leave 'em this spread. But I grew up on a sharecropping spread in East Texas. So I know what land is worth and how hard it is to call any your own. In another year, I'll own this whole quarter section and the water under it, freehold, to stay or sell. I reckon I'll sell. Raising horses is tedious as hell."

Longarm nodded. "I get the picture. You were smart to hang on to your homestead claim if it's almost proven. You say your man was bushwhacked?"

She put the cake down, went back to see if the coffee was warm enough, and brought the pot to table with a tray of cups and saucers. "That's what the sheriff said. I wasn't there. It happened out in No Man's Land, about a day's ride to the south. I don't know what he was doing on Double W range, neither. But that's where he was when someone blowed him off his horse. Horse come home alone, of course. So I called in the sheriff of Baca County. Had to ride all the way to Springfield to get him, and then he didn't want to look for my missing husband in the strip, at first. Finally got him to send some deputies out. They found my man—what the carrion crows had left of him. They asked, polite, at the Double W. But of course nobody over there had anything to say about a dead man on their range."

She spread the fixings and started slicing cake as she added, soberfaced, "I still say they was the ones. Sheriff's boys was just afeared of questioning old Colonel Calhoun personal."

She poured coffee for them both and sat down across from him, adding in a brighter tone, "Oh, well, my man left me well fixed. Thanks to my water tank being the only one about, the horses don't stray far. I sold a couple just the other day. Come to think on it, *they* was lawmen, too."

That was a lot more interesting indeed than her feud, justified or not, with some local power. Longarm asked, "Do tell? They told me over to the west a couple of riders came by, trailing someone."

"My God, you didn't stop at the Hawkins spread, did you? They're all crazy as bedbugs over there! I hope that nasty Hawkins gal, Shirly Ann, didn't try to attack you."

He smiled. "Not exactly. But I can see, now, why her Pa came back from visiting you filled with birdshot."

She grimaced and said, "The old fool has mighty busy hands. But I reckon I larnt him I was more particular than he hoped. Those white trash don't bother me as much as Colonel Calhoun, to the east, does. Pa Hawkins is only after a little slap and tickle. Colonel Calhoun wants my *water rights!*"

"Yeah. Water out here is harder to come by than some other pleasures. But let's get back to those so-called lawmen. Did they show you any I.D.?"

She thought, and shook her head. "I don't recall 'em offering and I was too polite to ask. They acted decent and they paid good money for a pair of ponies. They left their own jaded mounts as part of the bargain, so I come out way ahead. I made forty dollars clear. The mounts they left were as good as the ones they took. I'll show 'em to you later, if you like."

"They ain't as important to me as the ones they rode off on. What sort of ponies did they leave here aboard—and, while we're at it, what did *they* look like?"

She took a bite of cake and washed it down with coffee. "One gent was tall and thin," she said. "the other shorter and huskier-built. They just looked like regular cowboys—neither especially ugly nor particularly pretty." She stared

68

thoughtfully over the rim of her cup at Longarm. "Neither was as nice-looking as you. I sold 'em a dapple gray and a roan, both geldings. I offered 'em a nice bay stud I've saddle-broke, but the tall one said a stud could get a rider in too much trouble on strange range."

"He's likely worked as a cowhand at least once, then. Who did they say they were looking for? Latimer?"

"No, of course not. Who'd be looking for a federal land agent?"

"Me, for one. My office sent me down here to find out why he never came home with all the range fees he was supposed to collect. Uh—don't take this personal, Miss Betty, but could you show me your grazing permit, if it ain't too much trouble?"

She looked blank. "What range permit? I *paid* him, damn it!"

"I'm sure you did. But didn't he give you a paper to show for it?"

"Oh, I remember now. Mr. Latimer said he was out of forms but that the check I made out to him would serve as my receipt when the bank sent it back to me, canceled out."

Longarm took a sip of coffee. Her cake was dreadful. He swallowed to sort his thoughts, since talking in circles could be tedious. In truth, he didn't know if the land office was that sloppy or not. He hadn't gotten around to studying the typed onion skins Billy Vail had given him on the missing man. He asked, "Did you make out your check to Latimer, personal, or to the Bureau of Land Management in Washington, Miss Betty?"

"Neither. The check was made out to the land office up in Denver. Mr. Latimer made it out, so I just signed it."

He tried to look noncommittal, but she was a sharp-eyed gal. She asked, "Why? Is something wrong, Custis?"

He said, "Don't know. Have to send me some wires about it first. How far is the nearest town east, where a man might find a telegraph office?"

"You mean close to the strip? That's a ride indeed. There's

69

no towns *in* the strip, of course. Liberal, Kansas, lies just above the line, where the Rock Island Pacific cuts down to cross No Man's Land."

He whistled under his breath. He'd studied his survey map enough to know what she meant about a long ride. The Kansas railroad town was close to a hundred miles away. He drank some more coffee as he chewed that over in his mind. If he detoured north, he'd waste about as much time. If he pressed on to Liberal, stopping to jaw with folk along the way, he wouldn't be able to wire the office before the end of the week. But meanwhile he might stumble over anything, and he wasn't sure what it would mean if Denver confirmed his suspicion that Latimer was a lazy drunk who kept piss-poor records. The gal was right that her canceled check would sooner or later prove she'd paid somebody for something, and the government had nothing else to sell down here but grass.

He put down his empty cup, and Betty Harris refilled it promptly. He said he'd be proud to drink another, but it was getting late and he had to study on moving on.

"You said you wanted to look at the horses those other lawmen left in my corral," she said. "Besides, it's getting late, and I wouldn't advise you to ride for the Double W this late. Why don't you do her in the morning, when Colonel Calhoun sends his ugly crew out to cull the beef?"

"It's only about three, Miss Betty."

"I know. The ride will take you to nigh sunset, and you'd come riding in looking spooky with the sun behind your back. I know some say *I'm* spooky, but Colonel Calhoun's a really proddy old scoundrel, and there's no saying what might happen. He's made enemies on every side, and since that latest killing—"

"What killing, ma'am?" Longarm cut in, frowning with renewed interest.

She shrugged. "Oh, you know. The man who got killed further east. I don't know the details. I don't jaw much with my surly neighbors. But some hands riding west a few days ago stopped for coffee, and as we jawed they mentioned a

70

man had been killed on the open prairie, somewheres east. That's all I know. They hadn't seen it, neither. Just heard some folks gossiping about it."

He didn't ask her to elaborate, knowing she couldn't. He'd find out more as he got closer to the scene—if anyone had been killed at all. Drifters were always jawing about things they didn't know beans about. It made a lawman's job mighty tedious.

Betty saw that he didn't want any more coffee, so she rose and said, "Come on. I'll show you the horses you asked about and we can get some oats for your own."

He followed her out to the corral. As they approached, most of the ponies came over to the rail to get their noses patted. Longarm was beginning to see how one gal could eke by here, once her man had built things right and left her the horses to make pets of. He approved of her methods to a point. Longarm was too old a hand with horses to believe in spoiling the dumb brutes, but her pampering sure beat chasing them in a thin dress and bare feet.

Two horses, both bays, held back at the far end of the corral. She pointed at them with her chin and said, "That's them. As you see, they ain't used to living with us yet, but they're both good mounts."

Longarm nodded as he looked them over. One had a faded U. S. brand, the other none. They figured to read as livery hacks, still serviceable enough for casual riding but not up to anything more serious. The long-in-the-tooth cavalry horse had either been sold off as government surplus or stolen so long ago it was none of his business.

She stopped patting their noses and led him around to the barn. There was a neat stack of feed sacks just inside the door and one corner was filled with loose hay. Spooky Widow Harris patted a feed sack, passed on to flop down in the hay, and said, "Help yourself. Anything you see here is yours for the asking."

He figured one sack of oats would be as much as his spare could pack with the water and possibles. He turned to tell her so and noticed that she'd spread her legs and was

71

slowly drawing up her skirts, smiling boldly up at him as she asked, "See anything you like?"

He sure could, for she had nothing under that thin dress but herself, and now the skirt was all the way up, exposing her for full inspection. Longarm wasn't sure what a gent was supposed to say at a time like this, so he just skimmed his hat away, unfastened his gun rig, and dropped between her open thighs on his knees as he unbuttoned his shirt and fly. She closed her eyes and lay back with a hungry sigh. All he had to do was lower himself into her. As he did, her eyes popped open and she gasped, "Oh, you're taller than I thought!"

Then she wrapped her arms and legs around him and they swapped tongues and other parts until they'd both come, hard and fast. When he paused to get his breath back, she sighed. "It's much nicer in a bed with everything off. You do mean to stay the night, don't you, darling?"

He said, "I do now. But the house is far away and I'm still hard as a rock."

She laughed, rolled him off her, and slipped the thin dress off over her head as he finished shucking. She was right. It felt a lot nicer to resume the procedure stark naked in the hay. She'd looked skinnier in that dress, even screwing, but her naked torso was built well enough to be put in a museum with the other marble goddess gals.

But, while some women seemed to want a man to put them on a pedestal, old Betty liked to be treated raw and rough. She used plain Anglo-Saxon verbs as she suggested new positions. He might have known from the way she'd been singing in the bath just before she spotted him that she was a natural-loving bawd who just plain liked to fuck and wasn't shy about saying so. It made quite a contrast to the equally horny but more refined strawberry blonde he'd had last. He meant to enjoy this hot brunette to the full.

He humped her dog-style in the hay, noticing how specks of strawdust clung to her sweaty back and buttocks as he threw it to her from behind. She arched her spine to take it all. She groaned and said, "Oh, *do* it! Fuck me as hard as you can!"

He fired in her, held it still, and fingered her to glory as her internal contractions told him she was almost there too. She moaned and fell away, gasping. "Have you ever had a French lesson, honey?" she asked.

"Sure, but why don't we cool off a spell."

"You're right. We're both all messy. Let's go bathe in the tank."

He wasn't sure he wanted to. It was still broad day outside and he'd already caught her in the tank once today. But, hell, how many strangers passed such a remote spread on any given afternoon?

They held hands and ran, laughing, out to the big water tank. He helped her over the side, then rolled in to splash beside her. The water was up to his lower ribs and floated her tits just right as he held her close and they kissed, rubbing one another's privates clean. Then, since her wet fondling had renewed his ardor, he braced her back against the corrugated iron and proceeded to do it to her right, standing in the cool water. She raised her thighs and let them almost float as she held them wide for him, clinging to him with her wet, slippery arms. The contrast of the cold water and her warm interior felt funny but nice as he moved in and out of her. He came, and decided he might as well keep going, for there couldn't be a nicer way with such a pretty and willing partner.

He heard a nicker and looked up to see that his fool mount, Browny, had busted loose and was coming over to join them. Longarm figured he wanted a drink. He laughed and said, "Howdy, Browny. I should chide you for pulling that half-hitch free, but it's my own fool fault for forgetting you out in the hot sun all this time."

The gelding shoved his muzzle in the water and started inhaling as if he hadn't been watered in a week. "Go ahead. We're busy," Longarm said, and started moving in Betty again.

73

She had a better view over his bare shoulder than he did. She suddenly stiffened in his arms and said, "Oh, shit! Someone's coming from the east!"

Longarm whipped out of her and turned in the deep water to stare in the same direction. Two mounted men had reined in on the skyline. One sat tall in his saddle, the other less so. He asked Betty, "Double W hands?"

"I don't think so," she said. "They look like the two men who stopped the other day for horses. Those are the horses I sold them, too."

Longarm reached carefully for Browny's harness, knowing this was one hell of a time to spook a horse. He held Browny's head and murmured, "Easy, boy. I sure forgive you for busting loose now. And if we ever see another apple, it's all yours!"

As the mysterious riders made up their minds to come down the slope, Longarm reached out a long naked arm, caught some mane, and pulled the gelding around so he could get at the saddle gun handing from the off side.

He did so just in time. A bullet spanged off the water near them. Betty screamed and ducked under, which was mighty sensible thinking, for the second round splashed water and holed the tank right where her head had just been.

Longarm whipped the Winchester around, levered a round in the chamber, and stood his ground—or water—to fire back as they both rode in. His first round emptied the taller one's saddle. The shorter one had sudden second thoughts and reined in. But, as he spun his mount, Longarm put a rifle ball in him, too.

Their horses ran off back up the hill as Longarm waded to the far side, braced the Winchester over the rim, and asked Betty, who'd just come up for air, if she'd be kind enough to run and get their duds from the barn while he covered the men on the ground.

"I'm naked!" she protested.

"Don't worry," he said. "I'll shoot again if either one peeks. Shake a leg, girl! There's no telling who all may

74

have heard the gunfire, and I don't want to meet no *more* folks till I have my pants on."

Betty rolled over the far edge and ran for the barn. While he waited, Longarm detected no sign of life from either of the figures lying in the grass. That didn't mean much. He wouldn't have moved with a man holding a gun on him, either.

Betty came back with his duds and gunbelt. She'd forgotten his boots, but he noticed that she'd slipped into her dress in the barn. He said, "Good. Take Browny's reins and move back to the house. I'll join you directly, Lord willing."

As she moved with the gelding out of range, Longarm dressed enough to matter, covering the downed riders with his Winchester all the while. The grass stubble hurt his bare feet as he moved out to have a better look at them. He came to the short one first. There was no point in jawing with a man who'd taken a .44-40 in one ear and out the other, so he moved on to where the first one he'd shot lay face down in the grass. Longarm rolled him over on his back with a foot and saw he was still breathing. "Howdy," he said. "I understand you boys have been looking for someone. Could I be the one?"

The tall rider groaned. "Where the hell did you get that gun, Longarm? When we seen you swimming bare-ass with that gal, we thought..."

"I know what you thought, and since you know my handle, I know who you boys was sent after. Now all we have to settle is who sent you, right?"

"You got us all wrong, pard. We're lawmen, too. We wasn't after you. We was after an outlaw calt Lefty."

"No, you weren't, for I gunned Lefty back in Trinidad some time ago, and every lawman in town heard about it. You're wasting time trying to fun me, old son. I can see you're hit bad, but I don't mean to do a thing about it until you tell me something sensible."

"I think I'm hulled through at least one lung, Longarm.

I need a doc. I'll tell you all about it when I'm feeling more up to breathing. Right now it hurts like hell, and if you don't get me a doc ..."

Longarm swore, dropped to one knee, and started going through the dying man's pockets. The man on the ground gasped and said he was hurting him. Longarm said, "Too bad. You were out to hurt me. Let's see, now, you got an old hunting license made out to one Millard Greenwich. It's likely a real one. Ain't it a caution how easy it is for a drifter who needs I.D. to find such things as expired permits after they're throwed away?"

"Longarm, I sure feel awful. How come the sun ain't shining all of a sudden?"

"Must be fixing to rain. All right, mister. I've been considerate of your injured feelings up to now. But you're going to tell me who sent you after me, or it's going to smart like hell."

"I can't tell you, Longarm."

Longarm put the thumb of his free hand against the wounded man's left eye, pressed down hard, and said, "Sure you can, unless you like to hear eyeballs popping like crushed grapes, you son of a bitch!"

"Ow, Jesus, stop! You're *killing* me!"

"There's a lot of that going around of late. Who sent you after me? I ain't got all day, and neither have you."

There was no reply. Longarm stopped when he saw the fool was either unconscious or dead. He felt the base of the victim's throat and sighed. "When you're right you're right, old son. The only true words I got from you was that I was killing you. I reckon I made you gasp too hard on all that blood in your chest."

He straightened up and walked back to the house. As he approached, Betty came out. "What happened? Is it over?" she asked.

"For now it is. I'm looking for my boots and a shovel. Their horses will likely come home for supper, since they know this is the best place to eat for miles. I'll tidy up the rest of the mess I just made."

"You don't mean to bury them on my land?"

"Nope. They were killed federal, so I'll bury 'em federal, just over the line on federal range. I'll note it on my map, in the unlikely case anyone ever wants the son of bitches again."

She brightened. "Oh, good. I'll put our supper on while you take care of things out here. You . . . you still mean to spend the night here, don't you, darling?"

Longarm thought, shrugged, and said, "Tell you what, honey. You take my ponies in, unsaddle and feed 'em, and we likely have us a deal."

She clapped her hands. "I'll water and rub them down as well. Then I mean to fill you full of food and rub *you* down some, too!"

Longarm nodded. "That's what I just agreed to, old pal."

Chapter 8

Longarm had meant to get an early start the next morning, but what with one thing and another—finding out if a brunette was as inspiring as a strawberry blonde spread-eagled naked across a kitchen table, and a couple of other notions Betty said she needed to remember him by—he didn't get far enough to matter before nine. He tried to rest up some as he rode on at a sedate walk. The Spooky Widow Harris had said she'd never forget him, and he doubted he'd be fit to meet another friendly gal for a least a week.

So it was just as well that an ugly old man was seated on a rocker by the door when Longarm rode into the Double W a few hours later.

The ugly old man was wearing a shiny black suit and fancy Texas boots. He had one boot up on a veranda post as he rocked himself, regarding Longarm with distaste. As Longarm started to dismount, the old man spat and called out, "Keep riding, boy. We ain't hiring, and the Double W don't feed saddle tramps."

Longarm dismounted anyway, and the old man stood up warily. Longarm said, "Simmer down, Colonel Calhoun. I'm the law. I don't care if you want to feed me or not. I heard what a neighborly son of a bitch you was, so I had a pal make me some sandwiches this morning."

"Nobody calls me a son of a bitch and lives, you son of a bitch!"

"Well, I just did, and you just did, and since we're both still alive, I'd say we were even and we ought to let it stand at that. To save you a lot of tedious bluster and brag, they call me Longarm, and I could bluster and brag worse than you, if I was such a brainless shit."

Colonel Calhoun's jaw dropped. He called out, "Junior! Git out here and stomp this loco maniac afore I has a stoke!"

The door opened and a man built like a railroad locomotive came out to scowl at Longarm. "You called, Pappy?"

Longarm said, "Junior, get back in the house. This is grown-up talk, and your old man don't really aim to lose you so young."

Junior spouted like a whale and dropped a ham-sized hand to the old single-action .36 conversion he wore strapped to his leg for some fool reason. He gave up on the notion when he saw Longarm's .44 muzzle staring unwinkingly at his dumb face. "Pappy?" Junior whimpered.

Colonel Calhoun said, "Just go in the house and shut the door gentle, boy. I can see we may have misjudged our visitor, but I'm sure he aims to be friends. Ain't that right, Longarm, *amigo?*"

Longarm didn't answer or lower his gun until Junior had crawfished back into the house. Then he turned to the older man. "That's better. Sit down."

Colonel Calhoun did as he was told. "I'd heard the name, now that I study on it," he told Longarm. "Didn't make the connection till I saw that gun appear by magic in your paw. How come you're so surly, son?"

"I ain't your son. I can be polite with polite folks. But

I've met you before, and it saves time to settle who's scared of which right off."

"Longarm, no offense, but I disremember us ever meeting up afore."

"Sure we have. There's a big bullfrog like you in every little county puddle. You all found while playing in the sandpile as kids that most folks scare easy. But I never liked bullies when I was little. I stopped taking shit off them before I started shaving regular."

"You sure must get in a lot of fights, Longarm."

"Not as many as you might think. If your name was Clay Allison or King Fisher this conversation might have gone more thoughtsome. But since I never heard of you till yesterday, I knew you were just a run-of-the-mill bullfrog. Now that we've got that settled, I got some questions. Two riders rode this far east or farther, then turned back. One rode a gray and the other a roan. Tell me about 'em."

Colonel Calhoun shrugged and replied, "Ain't much to tell. I mind the boys you mentioned. They didn't stop here, so we didn't find out how tough they was. They stopped one of my hands, out on the range to the south. He was riding alone, so he had to be polite. They asked him had he seen a tall cuss in denims riding solo with a pinto and a bay. Since I can see both your ponies right behind you, I'd say you was in trouble, Longarm."

Longarm said, "Not anymore. I got another question. I'm looking for Hiram Latimer, the land agent. Has he been by of late?"

Colonel Calhoun chuckled and spat. "Not lately. I run the rascal off last time he tried to sell me my own damn grass."

"You what? How the hell are you grazing the strip without a government permit, Colonel?"

"Same way I always has. I run the cows out and they feed their fool selves. Old Latimer did come by to pester me about that. Like I said, I run him off. Told him it'd be a cold day in hell when I paid for range I took from Comanche, personal."

80

"Well, now that we're talking polite, Colonel, it's my duty to tell you that a man can get in trouble with the government, taking that attitude."

The old man shrugged. "That's what Latimer said. I run him off my land anyways. I ain't afraid of your damn Yankee government. I met the sissies at Pittsburgh Landing and I'm still here. Told Latimer he'd need as many men as Grant had there before I'd pay for grass the Good Lord planted for all comers in the first place."

"Don't you hold with property rights at all, Colonel?"

"Sure I do. A man's entitled to all the property he can keep others from taking away from him. I know what Latimer said about his Uncle Sam claiming title to the range to the south, but I ain't seen anyone in stars and stripes down there. Ain't seen nobody, not even Comanche, since I run some off when I come out here after the War. Until the land is settled sensible, it's meant to be grazed, and my cows are as hungry as any."

The man was a fool as well as a blusterer. But a lot of old timers were like Colonel Calhoun and Longarm didn't have time to convey the advantages of civilization to the squatter. It was up to the land office to evict him if he hadn't even filed a homestead claim under his soddy and windmill. Longarm said, "Tell me just how serious you ran Latimer off."

The old man laughed. "Hell, we never *hurt* him. Just shot some dust up between his pony's hooves. He got the message he wasn't welcome and rode off, yelling he'd be back. He never done so, though. He must not have been as mule-headed as you. It's been a year or more since last I laid eyes on the son of a bitch. Say, you want some coffee, son? I admires a man with guts. Like you said, they're hard to find. So us mean old birds gets lonesome. Come on in and set a spell whilst I tell you about the War."

Longarm said he knew about the War, mounted up, and rode on. Calhoun was as crazy an old crank as Betty had said. But he hadn't tried to run a woman alone off her homestead, and he couldn't have done much to Latimer if

81

he hadn't seen him for at least a year. Latimer had only been missing for about a month. The old man or one of his hands might or might not know something about the killing of Betty's husband. But it was a local matter, the local sheriff had investigated, and it was a mite late to poke about in crimes Billy Vail hadn't sent him out to look into.

He had enough on his plate with the murder of Latimer— if Latimer had been murdered. He swore and started to rein in as he remembered he'd forgotten to ask the old bastard if any of his hands had heard of a more recent killing farther east. Then he decided not to. Folks even farther east would likely know more, and talking to the old bastard without hitting him was a chore.

He clucked the pony he was riding into a trot, anxious now to get somewhere sensible. Reb Richardson had said he'd heard of a federal man getting killed down here somewhere. If drovers just passing through had heard it, someone local must have told them. Longarm needed someone who could fill in more details.

Longarm cursed himself again for not having picked up some chaps. The colonel's hell-for-leather attitude about open range had turned the land around his spread into damn near solid chaparral. Longarm kept spooking longhorns, wild and wary as deer, but they didn't make him as uneasy as a certain prickle at the nape of his neck that kept him reining in and looking back.

There was nothing to see behind him once he had the Calhoun windmill out of sight. But Longarm had been trailed before. He couldn't say what it was that told a man there were eyes staring at his back, but he'd saved his own life more than once by sensing them just in time.

This is mighty spooky, old son, he told himself. *You're out in the middle of nowhere much and there's not a damn thing in sight. You gunned the rascals who come after you from Trinidad, and whoever sent 'em couldn't have sent a whole damn army. Do you reckon you're suffering from a case of the proddies?*

Way off to the southwest he saw dust rising. Someone

82

was riding fast across the dried-up range. You didn't need a crystal ball to figure one or more of Colonel Calhoun's riders were chasing cows. The old fool had said they were rounding up for market. The dust rose too far off to concern an innocent just passing through. Anyone closer was moving too slow to raise dust and too low to be seen against the skyline. The brush was higher than it should have been, but not that high. None of the bushes around Longarm rose higher than his poor denim-clad knees. A man on foot could hunker down sudden, but nobody aboard a bronc could be close enough to matter. Longarm heeled Paint into a trot, pulling Browny after them as he muttered, "If anybody's trailing us afoot, let's make the bastard *work* at it!"

He felt better after he'd trotted a couple of miles and spied another windmill in the distance. He knew that a determined Digger Indian could keep up with a trotting horse indefinitely, but you hardly ever found a Digger on this side of the mountains. Such Plains Indians as might still be about didn't cotton to walking or running any more than most white men.

He topped a rise, reined in, and looked back. The sun was high and the heat shimmered everything back there. He saw movement everywhere, but nothing that he could say for certain was a ducking head. He shrugged. *Junior, maybe,* he thought. *He looked mean and stupid and you did sort of hoorah him. He had long legs, too. But, hell, how far could a moose like that keep up?*

He rode on the next spread. Like the others in the neighborhood, it consisted of a soddy and such nesting near the base of an older and lower sunflower water pumper. There was a veranda built along the south wall of the soddy. As Longarm rode in, a gent in faded Levi's and a sun-bleached straw hat stepped out of the shade to stare thoughtfully at him. The tall lawman waved his free hand to show that he didn't have a gun in it. As he came within earshot, he called out, "Hold your fire. I'm the law."

The settler called back a welcome and an invite to coffee, water, and such. As Longarm reined in by the house he saw that the man was a nice-looking young gent. An old lady sat rocking on the veranda, smoking a corncob pipe. The settler said his name was Conway, the old lady was his granny, and his wife, Sue Ellen, would be out directly with coffee. Conway said he'd lead the horses around to the shady side and give them some water and cracked corn. Longarm thanked him, went over to the veranda, and took off his hat to the old woman, who invited him to sit. There was no other chair, so he sat on the edge of the plank veranda. The old lady made him tell her who he was, where he'd come from, and where he was going. Longarm did so, leaving out a few details.

A pretty little gal sporting gingham and a shy smile came out to hand him a tin cup of Arbuckle and a tin plate of bread and jam. Then she scooted back inside before Longarm could finish thanking her. He could see why he hadn't been invited inside. Some nester gals were spooky as quail around strangers, not being used to seeing many.

Granny chuckled and told Longarm the gal was expecting and that the house was a mess. Longarm said he was right comfortable where he was. He waited a spell for the husband to come back, but Granny said he was likely out back fixing the windmill. "Do tell?" Longarm said. "It was spinning pretty good as I rode in."

The old woman said, "It's spinning, but it ain't pumping enough to matter. Nothing's coming up outten the ground but a trickle of muddy. My grandson don't know if it's a worn-out washer or a low water table. It's been mighty dry of late. It's a good thing we don't keep much livestock. Just a pony and the mule team. We're thinking about a milk goat, after the baby comes. But we'll manage, long as any water comes up at all."

Longarm washed down some bread and jam with the coffee before he replied, "No offense, ma'am, but if you ain't running stock on the range all about, it sure looks overgrazed."

"That's 'cause it *is,* sonny. That infernal Double W has its cows all over creation. We only have this quarter section to call our own. Colonel Calhoun says we staked it on his range, the old fool."

"I noticed he was sort of piggy about land others held title to from the land office, ma'am. Have you folk had trouble with him?"

She snorted in disgust. "He's mostly bluff. Sent that big, dumb son of his over to scowl at us when we first settled here a couple of years ago. My grandson scowls pretty good, too, so nothing come of it. Us Conways don't bully worth mention."

"I thought you folk talked sort of West-by-God-Virginia, ma'am. I took them for blusterers, too. Still, the colonel mentioned running Comanche off, and that Widow Harris on the far side says someone gunned her man a spell back."

Granny Conway shrugged and said, "I doubt the colonel ever saw Comanche one. He just likes to talk. Nobody else has ever had Injun trouble in these parts since the cavalry showed the rascals who was boss a few years back. As to who might have gunned Artie Harris, you can take your pick from a mighty long list. He was a mighty untidy neighbor." She spat. "Can't say much for his widow, neither. You say you met up with her. Did she trifle with you, sonny?"

Longarm shook his head in a silent lie. He'd thought old Betty made love like a gal who got a lot of practice. But, what the hell, she'd had a bath just before he met her. He asked about the Hawkins family he'd first met. "Trash," Granny said. "If that skinny daughter of Pop Hawkins ever got you alone, you'd have been ruint. They say she's got the clap. Likely caught it off her brothers."

Longarm grimaced in distaste. The old gal sure was a mean-mouthed old gossip. But gossips had their uses to a curious lawman, so he asked her if the two riders on the roan and the gray had come this far. She said they hadn't. He asked if she knew Hiram Latimer, and she said she did.

"He comes by here as he makes his rounds. Can't say when we last seen him last. We don't graze nothing, so we don't buy grazing permits," she told Longarm.

Longarm finished the last of the bread and jam, washed it down, and asked, "Could you tell me what you do raise, if it ain't too personal?"

She said, "It ain't personal. It's grain. We tried wheat the first year. Got dusted out. But barley seems to grow well enough. The kids have nigh forty acres planted this year, over to the north, ahint all that infernal brush. My grandson's been clearing the brush betwixt chores. The Double W made a hell of a mess out of the land before we filed claim on her. But the soil's still fertile, once you get down to her, and the brush burns better than cow chips."

Longarm didn't say anything.

She nodded. "I knows what you're thinking, sonny. None of you cowboys think this land is worth farming. But it can't be helped. My grandson can't ride too good and we can't afford the hired help a cattle operation would take. Besides, we're Sooners."

Longarm had never heard the term before, and said so.

"We're playing a waiting game," she explained. "All that federal land to the south figures to be opened to homesteading as soon as we elect somebody sensible in Washington. The Indian Nation's applied for statehood. But, as none of the civilized tribes dwell this fur west, white folks mean to have it. The strip is the last big hunk of pure unsettled land left."

"I can see that, ma'am. At the risk of giving away state secrets, I can tell you it don't seem likely they'll open up the strip of homesteaders in the near future. I wouldn't bet on it for a good ten years or more. Besides, you already have your claim, here on the Colorado side of the line."

She said, "A lot *you* know, sonny! A quarter section of land this fur west ain't worth warm spit as a money-making proposition. This homestead's in *my* name, as a War widow. Soon as land to the south opens up, my grandson means to grab a quarter section for him, a quarter section for his wife, and a quarter section for the kids as is coming. In ten years or less they'll have enough kids to claim a whole *township*.

Meanwhile, as we hold a quarter section smack on the line . . ."

"I get the picture. You'll have a good head start on other land rushers. Most as come will fail to prove their claims when they get dusted out the first year. It takes a head start with tools, cash, and water to prove a homestead on dry prairie."

She cackled. "There you go. Us Sooners who got here soonest just have to run our fence lines and water lines due south."

Longarm put down the empty cup, shot a silent question as he took out a smoke, and, when the old lady nodded, lit up. He took a drag before he said, "This sooning business is interesting, now that I study on it, ma'am. Aside from you folk, the Calhouns, the Widow Harris, and them trashy Hawkinses to the west might be considered Sooners, too. Between you, you control a fair length of the border. If you got together, you'd be in a fair way to keep out anyone aiming to land rush. You might even be able to make 'em pay for the privilege of lining up on Opening Day."

She shrugged. "That's what Artie Harris was talking about before someone gunned him," she said. "He was wandering about trying to organize some sort of such a notion. Leastways, that's what he *said* he was doing. Some said he spent more time trifling with neighbors' horses and womenfolk than he should have. You knows, of course, that half the horses at the Tumbling H has no proper bill of sale on 'em?"

Longarm frowned. Betty had been sort of wild, but he hadn't seen her as a horse thief. If her late husband had been, it was a mite late for the law to worry about it. He said, "Well, I can see how a man with such a reputation could have got gunned, whether innocent or guilty. And it ain't the case I was sent to work on, ma'am. Could we get back to Latimer, the land agent?"

"He was a shiftless drunk, but harmless," she said flatly.

He nodded. "I've heard as much elsewhere, ma'am. I

heard he, or someone who sounds like him, got gunned down here, too. But nobody seems to be able to locate whomsoever in time and space."

"Well, sonny, as you can see, there's plenty of space out here. As to time, the Latimer boy was alive and well the last time he set right where you're sitting and drunk coffee from that same cup. It was—let me see—about a month ago, I reckon. He left here to ride due east. Said the Slash Bar Seven owed Uncle Sam for grass. They'd know better than me if he ever made it that fur. The Slash Bar Seven's mayhaps forty miles east."

He whistled silently and asked if there were any spreads between here and the next.

She shook her head. "Nope. Water's *pizened* betwixt here and there. Plenty of grass, but bad water. You'll come on what looks like a water hole, about twenty miles out. Don't let your ponies take one sip. There's something wrong with the water in that old buffalo wallow. If you drill a well within miles of it, the results can be fatal."

He thanked her for the advice, got to his feet, and went around to get his ponies. Off to the north he saw young Conway and two mules. They were either ploughing or, more likely, cultivating some barley they'd drilled in earlier. Longarm waved, and the sodbuster waved back. Longarm switched saddles again and rode Browny out, leading Paint. As they left the homestead, he looked up at the sun and saw they figured to be camping on open prairie that night. That didn't fret him. But after he'd ridden a couple of miles he started feeling eyes on the back of his neck again. *That* was starting to annoy the hell out of him.

Chapter 9

The sun was low but the light was still good when Longarm reined in on a rise to stare morosely down at a good-sized pond of standing water in a lower-than-usual draw ahead. He'd have figured out something was wrong, even without Granny Conway's warning. For the grass grew thick and lush in every direction, the chaparral had faded away, and the prairie looked unspoiled. That was how an experienced plainsman could tell bad water. If a water hole was any good, hooves would have trampled the banks all around it to bare dirt. Animals were good at finding water in dry country and they could smell when it was unfit to drink, too. So not even a jackrabbit had been near that water hole in some time.

Longarm grimaced. *Damn it, you sure could use a swim right now, too, old son,* he thought. *Wonder what ruined that water. You're on the wrong side of the Great Divide for alkali water. Lead salts, maybe. Lots of lead in the hills of the Indian Nation to the east. Seems far, but you never know how the rocks crop up under all this deep prairie soil.*

He decided to camp there. For, while the water might be bad, the grass all about was lusher than any he'd seen so far along the abused strip. He had oats and water for his mounts, but he knew that cow ponies relished grass to settle their guts.

Longarm liked the notion of camping out in the open, too. The feeling that they were being followed came and went. Whether he was just spooked, or whether the hairs on the back of his neck were smarter than the rest of him, he knew nobody could creep up close enough to matter across open ground.

He took a pair of tethering pegs from the packsaddle and drove them into the sod twenty paces apart, using the back of a hatchet that was lashed to his camping gear. The stakes drove hard, for the sod was tough and the soil below was baked like adobe. He tethered the ponies before removing stock and packsaddles and placing them a few feet apart on the grass between them. He unrolled his sleeping bag on the grass between the saddles. The he fed and watered the ponies well to settle them down, figuring that the bad water wouldn't pester them after they'd drunk the real thing.

He sat on the bedroll, Winchester on the tarp at his side, as he fished in his saddlebag for supper. A fire would be dangerous with the grass all about so tall and dry, even if he didn't hanker for some privacy after dark on the prairie. He opened a can of beans and a can of tomatoes. He got the cold beans down, used the tomatoes as a combined drink and dessert, and decided he was either full or too sick to care.

The sun went down, and the moon hadn't risen yet. Longarm wasn't sleepy. He sat on the bedroll, smoking a cheroot and counting shooting stars. The cloudless sky was filled with stars. Some looked close enough to reach up and grab.

Every once in a while one fell out of the sky, as stars

had a habit of doing on the High Plains in late summer. But after a while he lost interest. He'd been told as a boy that you got one wish every time you spied a shooting star. But he'd spied many a shooting star in his time, and he still wasn't rich, so he sort of doubted the notion.

He'd about decided to turn in when he noticed another glimmer of light to the west, between Paint's legs. It was too bright and too yellow for a low star. He frowned as he watched it grow brighter. He wet a finger to test the wind. It was coming from the west, and unless the recently set sun had decided to come back up, he was staring at a prairie fire, sure as hell!

He started gathering everything together as he kept an eye on the not-too-distant blaze. He'd just cinched the stock saddle back on Paint when he saw another light flare to the north.

Some son of a bitch is out to burn you dead, old son. For if that wasn't another match struck, yonder, they sure have mighty big fireflies out here!

He pulled up the stakes and led the ponies downslope, walking between them. *You can't outrun the breeze, but yonder water hole is wide and shallow. I hope these ponies remember what you told 'em about drinking there!*

He waded into the water hole, holding each pony by the snaffle to keep their heads up. Paint behaved herself, but Browny kept trying to lower his fool muzzle as he felt water above his dumb knees. Longarm shook his bit and growled, "Cut that out. I might have known a horse with no balls would have no natural instincts. That water's no good, you idjet!"

He waded out to the middle. The water came to Longarm's mid-thighs, so he didn't have to worry about getting more than the muzzle of his .44 wet. He swung the ponies around so that Browny was between him and the fireline. The skyline was well lit, now. Longarm could see clearly between the pool's edge and the fire. It was a big one, but it wasn't coming too fast, for the wind was mercifully gentle. The son of a bitch who'd started it had lit the brush and grass a quarter of a mile either way north and south. He was somewhere in the darkness beyond, and likely on foot, unless he rode a rabbit. Longarm had been looking back a lot that afternoon.

The fire crept closer, taking its time as it licked up grass as dry as mummy dust, but without a real wind to back its play.

Longarm could see that the fire line wasn't too thick as it slowly advanced. A wall of dirty orange smoke rose in its wake, screening anyone who might be on the far side. But Longarm knew that he and the ponies were illuminated to someone over there when a muzzle flash winked at them, dull orange in the smoke, and a bullet whizzed just above the saddle on Paint.

Longarm let go of Browny's harness, drew his .44, and fired across the empty saddle at the other's muzzle flash. Then, since he saw this was a losing proposition, Longarm filled the saddle with his butt, swung Paint's head to face the fire, and heeled her hard, yelling, "Powder River and let her buck!" as he rode right into the fire wall at a full gallop.

Paint didn't like it much, but a well trained wall cow pony did as she was told, and they only got singed a mite around the edges before they'd burst through the high, thin wall of flame and were going lickety split in a cloud of rising hot ash. The fire now behind them shed its light both ways, so Longarm could see a figure on foot, running like hell. Longarm guided Paint after him and fired one warning shot into the ash ahead of the bastard.

The running man didn't take the hint. He dropped to one knee, spun around to train the carbine in his hands at Longarm's black outline, and caught a second round of .44 with his teeth for his pains.

Longarm reined in above his fallen foe and dismounted for a better look. His round had blown teeth and brains out the far side of the arsonist's head, but there was enough left of his dead face for Longarm to make him out a total stranger.

Longarm holstered his gun and held Paint's reins in his other hand as he dropped to one knee in the warm ashes to pat the body down. The man was dressed cow and his wallet contained papers saying his name was Jerome MacSorley.

The name rang a distant bell. But, as the rascal was dead as well as a stranger, Longarm put the name in the back file of his mind as he found out what else the cadaver had to offer.

The late MacSorley had fifty-three dollars and change an underpaid public servant could use. His carbine was a .30-30 and his sidearm was an old single-action .38, so Longarm couldn't use his ammunition. He put the empty wallet back. Some local law might want to know who he'd been, if and when they found him. Longarm saw no need to own up to the killing, for filling out papers was tedious and the rascal wasn't anyone on his wanted list.

He said to the body, "Well, it was mighty interesting meeting up with you, you son of a bitch. You ran pretty good in them low-heeled boots, and I'd sure like to know why. But, as you're dead, we'll just say no more about it for now."

He started to lead the pinto back to the water hole, but as he turned away a shot rang out behind him. Longarm whirled, drew, and put another round in the man on the ground before a second round in the dead man's gunbelt went off under him.

Longarm laughed, sheepishly. *Them ashes he's roasting on are hotter than you figured,* he told himself.

They went back to the water hole. The fire had burned itself out in the lusher grass in the bottom of the draw, and it was dark once more. Browny nickered and came over to join them. Longarm took the gelding's lead, mounted Paint, and rode on. As the moon rose less than an hour later, he saw they were all alone on open range, so he reined in and made camp again. The spooked ponies would doubtless let him know if anything bigger than a horny toad came within a country mile, so Longarm caught a few hours' sleep before the sun woke him again.

Breaking camp only took a few minutes. He started to put the stock saddle on Browny. Then he saw the listless way the bay's head was drooping. He said, "I might have known you'd drink from that water hole, you poor fool. I sure hope you didn't drink enough bad water to matter."

Browny had. He made it through the day to about noon. But just as Longarm, standing in Paint's stirrups, could see a distant windmill, the gelding sank to the sod with a sad nicker and lay there like a whipped pup with his slavering muzzle between his outstretched forelegs. Longarm dismounted, stepped back to hunker down and examine the sick gelding's eyes, and muttered, "You sure was dumb, for a cow pony, and the boys at the Diamond K are going to be sore as hell about this."

He removed the packsaddle and took it over to Paint. "You can carry this as well if I walk the rest of the way, Paint. Your pard is done for, but they may sell us another at that windmill up ahead."

Longarm held her reins in his left hand to keep her from spooking as he drew his .44, took aim on the soft spot just over Browny's left eye, and put the poisoned bay out of his misery with a single shot. Paint flinched some, but he steadied her down as they trudged on toward the distant windmill.

It took forever to get there, but they made it. As he led Paint up to yet another soddy, he saw two she-male figures watching him from the shade of the veranda. He waved, walked the rest of the way in politely, and told the two gals who he was and why he was walking with two saddles on one pony. They said they were the Gump sisters, both giggling silly as they said so.

One silly sister was named Debbie and the other said to call her Billie. They were both nice-looking, in their silly way. Debbie was ash blonde and Billie's hair had more red in it. Debbie took Paint around to the corral to rest and water her as Longarm followed Billie inside for the coffee and grub they'd offered. The one-room soddy smelled like old cobwebs and cheap perfume mixed with lamp oil. Billie sat him down at a sort of table improvised from two planks across two barrels. She served him hot coffee and lukewarm hash, and said they'd be proud to sell him one of their horses whenever he was fixing to leave. She sat down across from him and added archly, "You don't want to leave just yet, for there's not another spread for forty miles either way, and you'll never make it anywhere before sunset catches you lonesome on the prairie."

Debbie came in, said Paint would likely live, and agreed that Longarm should stay a spell. A man could get the distinct notion they didn't have many visitors. He asked what they were doing out here all alone and Debbie said they were Sooners, too. "We're right near the trail north from Texas. We've got the only water for miles. You'd be surprised how profitable it is to water a herd of cows at two bits a head."

"No, I wouldn't, Miss Debbie. I used to drive cows. Two bits a head seems mighty steep," Longarm said.

"Not when there's no other water for miles and you want to drive 'em to market fat and sassy. We heard they was fixing to open up No Man's Land to settlers any day now. So we put all our savings together and come out last year to get in on the ground floor. We've each filed separate, of course, so we hold a half mile right along the borderline."

"Smart thinking. Meanwhile, what do you do to pass the time out here in the middle of nowhere?"

The sisters exchanged glances and giggled. Billie said, "From time to time folks pass by. A whole mess of cowhands just passed the other day, headed south." She frowned and added, "They said they couldn't stay."

"I'm sure sorry to hear that, Miss Billie. Would the outfit have been the Richardsons' Rocking X? I've a reason for asking."

Debbie shook her head. "No, the Rocking X passed days ago, driving north. We sold 'em a mess of water. But they acted in a hurry, too. Do you think we look ugly, Mr. Long?"

"Not hardly, but, as I once bossed some trail drives, I know you have to keep your hands and your cows moving. I know the Rocking X. Had words with 'em up Denver ways a few days ago. They told me some folks down here told 'em a land agent named Latimer had gotten killed, somewhere in the strip. You gals hear anything about it?"

Debbie giggled. "It was us as tolt 'em. They had to stay long enough for coffee as they watered their herd. We heard about it from *another* rider from the south. He stayed longer, the nice old thing. He told us a gent named Latimer got killed down to the Texas side of the strip. It wasn't him as figured it was Latimer the land agent. *We* figured it out, since we knew Hiram right well."

Her sister said, "All he ever wanted was likker, though. Ugly old coot."

Longarm nodded. "I heard he had a drinking problem. But that's not what I'm looking for him to ask about. He's sort of missing. You say a man by the same name was gunned to the south? I'd like to hear about that, ma'am."

The sisters exchanged glances. "How much is that worth to you, cowboy?" one of them asked.

"I'm not a cowboy, I'm the law. Finding out what happened to old Latimer's worth most anything within reason. I don't carry much loose change in my britches, ladies."

Billie stood up and said, "I reckon what you *do* carry in your britches will do well enough." As Longarm gaped at her, she slipped off her cotton dress and moved naked over to the brass bedstead in the corner.

"Wait for *me,* damn it!" cried her sister, jumping up to shuck her own dress as she scampered over to the same bed, giggling like a fool.

He decided they were both a mite feebleminded as they giggled at him from the bed across the room. But feebleminded or not, it was hard to say which had the nicest body. He grinned and rose, both ways, as he said, "Well, seeing as it's my duty to question folks, we'd best get down to brass tacks."

He joined them, sitting on the edge of the bed to start unbuttoning his duds. But the silly sisters both grabbed him to help. As Debbie removed his gunbelt, Billie unbuttoned his fly, hauled out what she found inside, and said, "Hot damn! Look what this one's *hung* like!"

Debbie must have approved, too. She got both feet on the dirt floor with Longarm's lap between her wide-spread thighs and simply lowered herself on his shaft, dog style. Her sister protested, "That's not fair! I seen it first!"

Longarm said nothing. He just lay on his back, getting undressed the rest of the way by Billie, who kissed him hot and hungry while her sister rode to glory on his erection.

He knew he'd feel ashamed of himself later. Billy Vail would never approve of a federal employee taking such shameful advantage of a pair of halfwits. But meanwhile, it felt grand. It was hard to remember that he'd left the last gal feeling so tired of women.

Despite a certain distaste at their forward ways and obvious pasts, Longarm could tell that neither had been with a man since last he'd been with another woman, so he forgave them both as Debbie popped her cork in a natural, no-nonsense way.

She rolled off his lap to flop on one side, sighing. "He's all your's, Billie. But make it snappy. I want him back."

That seemed fair. Longarm hadn't come yet. He rolled aboard Billie, old-fashioned, and started pounding her like hell. He came almost at once, but Billie was so hot she beat him there and yelled how good it felt. Longarm had just stopped in her to catch his second wind when the blonde started beating on his rump with her clenched fists, saying, "Now me! It's my turn again!"

He decided it sure was, as he mounted Debbie, for at this angle she was a totally new experience. It took them both longer to climax now, and by the time he'd satisfied Debbie, Billie was sitting on the small of his back, rubbing her darker thatch up and down his spine as she whimpered that she was dying from emptiness. He just had to roll off Debbie and aim it up as Billie lowered herself aboard and proceeded to screw the hell out of him, bouncing her soft breasts shamelessly as she slid up and down the maypole. Debbie grabbed one of Longarm's hands and tucked it in her own lap, pleading, "Jerk me off while you screw her!" The three of them came together, the two gals kissing and rubbing tits above him as he fired in one and explored the other to the knuckles.

After that, they all agreed it was time for a breather. So Longarm lay between them, sharing a cheroot with them like a peace pipe as one or the other fondled his limp shaft while he enjoyed the afterglow.

He waited until he saw that nobody was about to rape him for a spell, and asked again about the gunning of the gent named Latimer. Debbie put one of his hands in her lap again as she said, "We never said he was *gunned*. The way we heard tell, he got run over by a *train!* It was down near the Texas line. The Rock Island Pacific run him over and scattered him for a mile across the prairie."

The blonde couldn't say if Latimer had been riding or walking along the tracks at night when a locomotive had hit him fair and square with plenty of elbow room all around for any man with a lick of sense.

Longarm frowned and wondered aloud how a man could manage such a fool trick. Billie said, "He was likely drunk. Nobody in the engine cab expected to see a natural man standing smack on the tracks in the middle of open prairie, so they hit him doing fifty miles an hour, it's been said. You want this cigar back, honey?"

"Not hardly. Let's see, now. That track's one hell of a ways off, and even further if he got hit forty miles south of the Kansas line. Do you gals know if there's a town down there where someone might have more on the accident, or whatever?"

Debbie said the tracks crossed into Texas near a bitty town called Hitchland, where the locomotives stopped for

98

water just inside Texas after boring across the strip without stopping or even looking for drunks on the right of way. Longarm didn't answer. His teeth were too clenched, for Billie had tired of the cheroot and was trying to smoke his organ grinder. She always inhaled when she smoked, it seemed.

Debbie laughed, told her to get it good and hard, and started making love to Longarm's fingers some more as Billie swiveled around to present her rear to both their faces, legs wide and pink slit gaping as she sucked him hard and hot.

Longarm massaged her wet clit with his thumb. It seemed to pleasure her, but Debbie said, "Let *me* eat her," and proceeded to do so as Longarm kept fingering Billie's blonde box. It was nice to see that the sisters got along so well between manly visits. It looked dirty as hell. He groaned. He was fixing to come, so Billie removed her mouth and Debbie swung her hot box aboard it, still eating her sister as Longarm ejaculated in her. Hot from his fingering and the naughty, perverse way she was using her tongue, Debbie came almost at the same time. Then, as they all fell limp, Debbie yawned and said, "Let's get some sleep and start all over."

Longarm agreed, of course, but he said he had to make sure his last pony was all right. So neither silly sister protested when he got dressed and left them half dozing in one another's arms.

He went outside, walking sort of funny, and it seemed surprising that the sun was still so high. He found Paint, bare-backed and looking rested, in the corral. He spied another mare, a pretty buckskin with a white blaze and stockings, and seeing that the two of them seemed to be getting along, he said, "Well, Buck, I'll let you carry the packsaddle a spell, till Paint and me figure out how agreeable you are."

He saddled both ponies and led them around to the front of the soddy. He stepped inside, saw that the sisters were both sound asleep, and put forty dollars on the table without

99

disturbing them. He knew the buckskin wasn't worth that much, but it wasn't his money, and he hoped they wouldn't feel too disappointed about the deal when they awoke to find him gone.

He faced a lonesome night out on the prairie again, but his pecker could doubtless use the rest. He had one hell of a long ride ahead. And he was saddlesore before he even started.

Chapter 10

Longarm rode catty-corner to the southeast across No Man's Land, making fair time. Old Buck led better than Browny had. When he swapped saddles around four-thirty he discovered that she rode more responsively, too. He felt better about sharing most of the spoils from the late MacSorley's wallet now. His pal at the Diamond K would doubtless forgive him for losing Browny on them, now that he had a better cow pony to hand back to them in Browny's place.

He camped on a stretch of dead-flat open prairie as the sun was setting again. Out here the range had been spared the ravages of overgrazing and looked the way prairie was supposed to look at this time of year. The sod was too thick and the dusty dry grass all around too dangerous for a fire unless he wanted to peel back nine or more feet of sod. It wasn't worth the effort. He'd eaten almost-warm hash that kept repeating on him. So he settled for some more cold beans after watering the ponies and setting them to grazing at the ends of the stake ropes.

He was tired enough, now. But there was still enough light to read by, so he took out the papers on Latimer and decided to bone up on the rascal, not that there was a better than fifty-fifty chance he'd solved the vanishment.

He wound up even more disgusted with the missing fee collector by the time he had finished. Latimer was one of the no-goods left over from the corrupt Grant administration, when anyone who voted a certain way could get a government job. Latimer had been disciplined a lot and transferred from branch to branch of the land office, mostly for just plain goldbricking. Colonel Calhoun had said Latimer didn't take his job seriously. A man collecting money for Uncle Sam wasn't supposed to ride off just like that. Hardly anybody paid up willingly, and a federal agent was supposed to have more sand in his craw.

Latimer had been useless in other ways. He'd sired a little gal back East. The baby had been legitimate, thanks to the shotgun of the bride's pappy, most likely, but Latimer had deserted his pregnant bride before she'd given birth. There was a copy of the court papers ordering Latimer to support his deserted wife and kid. It was just as well the wife had remembered Latimer worked for Uncle Sam. Hardly any other boss would have made the rascal ante up a third of his monthly pay. He must have been left having to save up between drunks, for the record showed he could go a month or more between waking up in some trail-town drunk tank.

In other words, the missing man had been a shiftless skunk, and it was small wonder that it had taken even his office some time to notice he was missing. According to one of the last onion skins, Latimer's Denver boss, Waterford, had given him one last chance to shape up or ship out and he'd shown up more or less sober the last few times. Longarm decided that Waterford was far more tolerant than he was himself. There were lots of better men looking for a steady job, and the one they'd been wasting on Latimer was duck soup. All it called for was poking from spread to spread like a traveling drummer or any other bill collector. Latimer

102

had had no time clock to punch and no bugle calls to wake him up in the morning. It was a perfect job for a lazy man who could move at all.

Longarm put the papers away with a shrug, blew a smoke ring at the sunset, which was sort of pretty, and thought, *All right, if you find out in Hitchland that the same Latimer got run down by a train while wandering drunk along the tracks at night, there's no mystery left and nobody to arrest. Damn Billy Vail!*

He unrolled his sleeping bag, took off his boots and gun rig, and got in to see if he felt like sleeping yet. He didn't. He stared up at the colorful sky. *Hold on, now. There's still some missing pieces. If Latimer was killed open-and-shut accidentally, how come so many folks don't want you to look any deeper into the case? A mess of gunslicks and arsonists have been trying to stop your clock, old son. Let's study on why.*

He did so as the ponies cropped peaceably nearby and a night bird called out low and wistful in the gathering dusk. Unless the man who'd been hit by a train was some other Latimer, there were still too many loose ends. The Rock Island Pacific must know they had run over some damned somebody by now. Everyone else did. It was the duty of a halfway responsible railroad company to search for the next of kin, even when they killed a hobo.

The body had been identified as someone named Latimer, or nobody would be saying it was Latimer. They'd probably done so in Hitchland, Texas. He could see by his survey map that they had a Western Union wire running down along the tracks there. How come nobody had wired Denver about it? Was the whole town, even a small one, in cahoots with the gang that kept trying to stop the law from looking into the accident—or whatever it was?

It hardly seemed likely. Even the town drunk would have to be cut in for part of the loot, and how much loot could there be?

Latimer collected range fees paid by checks made out to his office. Assuming even a few stockmen had been fool enough to pay cash, not having bank accounts, Latimer could have been packing enough money to make it worthwhile for a smallish gang to kill him for it. But there was no way he could have packed enough to buy the services of assassins after paying off a whole damned town, from coroner to saloon swamper. Make that the *railroad*, too. The train crew couldn't all be related by blood to the law in Hitchland.

Longarm fell asleep making up lots of wires he meant to send if and when he got to a telegraph office. The next time he opened his eyes the sun was shining in them, so he got up, had a can of tomatoes for breakfast, and waited until he'd roused the dozing ponies and ridden on before he lit his first smoke for the day.

The morning air was crisp and the ponies were frisky, so he trotted the kinks out of their legs, resisting the temptation to lope. Loping was more comfortable, but not a good notion if one meant to ride all day, even switching mounts. He stood in the stirrups, trying to keep his tailbone from getting pounded as he ate up some miles the way it was easier on horses than on poor humans packing tailbones and kidneys inside. The steady chafing of the saddle between his legs jerked his old organ grinder hard. That was another disadvantage of riding at a steady trot. He smiled wistfully as he recalled that pretty breed gal he'd once ridden with at a trot, up Canada way. She said she'd never come that way before, either.

It didn't help his glands to daydream about past romantic moments, so he tried to concentrate on the mystery ahead. But the closer he got to Texas, the more it seemed as if he'd been sent on a snipe hunt. He wasn't a third of the way and he was already finding Latimer tedious as hell, dead or alive.

He rode until the sun said it was close to noon and he was studying on whether to have canned sardines or some more beans for his next meal when he spied dust on the horizon ahead, as he road Buck closer, leading Paint, he could make out a prairie schooner raising all that dust as it went lickety-split to the west, faster than any sensible driver would have wanted to.

He dropped Paint's lead and heeled Buck into a lope, saying, "Looks like we have to head off a runaway, Buck."

Buck was willing, but as the cow pony carried him to head the prairie schooner off at an angle, he saw that a woman in dusty black was holding the reins in one hand and lashing at her team with the other as if she had the devil incarnate chasing her.

Longarm looked back the way she'd come and saw nothing but dust starting to settle on the horizon far behind. He rode up beside the fast-moving little covered wagon and called out, "Howdy, ma'am. You're fixing to kill your team, you know."

When he saw that she was staring wild-eyed at him as though she were out of her head, he rode ahead, reached out, and grabbed the head harness of the near horse to stop it.

The team stopped willingly enough, even with the fool woman still switching at their rumps.

"Cut that out, ma'am," Longarm called.

But what stopped her was a young girl of maybe twelve, who ducked out from under the canvas to wrap her naked arms around her mother and sob, "Stop it, Ma! It's all right now. Just *stop* it, hear?"

Longarm saw that the rest of the little gal was naked, too, though he could only see her from the waist up as she leaned against the back of the wagon seat. As she took the whip from the older woman, Longarm rode closer, tipping his Stetson. The young gal gasped and covered her budding breasts with her hands as she ducked back out of sight.

The woman who'd been driving stared dully at Longarm from under the brim of her black sunbonnet. "We have to get away," she said.

Longarm said, "I'd say you *done* it, ma'am. There's nobody within miles. What spooked you—outlaws or Indians?"

"We have to get away," she repeated, vacant-eyed.

Longarm rode closer, climbed off Buck to board the wagon seat beside her, and took the reins gently from the numb fingers. "It's all right now, ma'am," he said soothingly. "I got my guns loaded and there's not a soul about but us."

She didn't answer. He saw that she was sort of pretty in a faded way, under all the dust on her clammy face. He leaned out to check and saw he'd said the simple truth. As his own two ponies proceeded to join her jaded team in cropping grass, Longarm called out, "Missy, inside, there, I sure wish you'd stick your head out and tell me what in thunder's going on. I hardly ever eat little gals. My name is Custis Long and I ride for the law."

The kid stuck her tow head and freckles out, staring wide-eyed at Longarm. "Are you a real lawman?" she asked.

"I am. Here, I'll show you my badge. Who was chasing you ladies just now? Or I should say a time ago? There's no dust rising within ten miles or more."

She said, "We had to get away from Pa."

He blinked. "You gals ran off and left the man of the house afoot on the lone prairie? That's mighty unusual behavior, missy—no offense."

"He's not my real Pa," she said. "Mamma married up with him a few months ago. We was going west to New Mexico. He said he had a job there."

"Well, he'll have a time getting there now. I don't mind telling you, us lawmen find family disputes mighty tedious to stick our noses into. No matter which side seems to make sense, the poor lawman gets in a bind when they kiss and make up after time calms everyone down a mite. How far back did you leave your stepdaddy?"

"I don't know. I was on the wagon bed, bawling. Ma was driving. I reckon it was a ways back."

Longarm glanced at the team ahead and said, "I'd say you were right, from the way those poor brutes are lathered. In another mile or so you'd have all been stuck. Had not I come along, this confused lady, here, would have run 'em both into the ground, and we're miles from the nearest anything."

"Well, we had to get away," the child said.

Her mother snapped partly out of her spell and gasped. "Oh, yes, we have to get away! Help us get away, sir! I never knew the man was such a monster till he had us at his mercy out here in...Where *are* we, sir?"

"*Nowhere*, like I just said, ma'am. But, as you can see, there's nobody here but us. So suppose you tell me what happened. Your daughter don't speak highly of her step-daddy. What's his problem, mean drunk?"

"He's a brute. He just raped my child."

The girl blushed. "Not all the way, Mamma. You stopped him in time, remember? He just tore my duds off. But I saved my virtue by keeping my legs crossed tight, like you told me."

Longarm whistled silently, wishing that he'd overslept. Now he was in for it, no matter what he did. As a paid-up peace officer, he had to enforce such laws as there might be on open federal land, and if trying to rape a twelve-year-old kid wasn't a federal offense, it ought to be. But, damn it, he knew how these infernal domestic cases could go, by the time you got anyone to trial.

He'd never seen the supposed rapist, let alone seen him trying to rape anyone. The two gals were bearing witness now, but if they changed their story later, as so often happened in such family disputes, the whole thing was a waste of time he didn't have to spare.

Billy Vail hadn't sent him all the way down here to keep no-good stepfathers from trifling with minors. It was happening all the time up in Denver, to hear the Denver police tell it. *They* found the charges got dropped eight times out of ten, too. Some wives would put up with an awesome amount of abuse just to stay married to a good provider. Most of the men doing time for incest-rape were out-of-work losers.

He asked the sensible daughter for more details. Her tale,

in a nutshell, was that her mother had climbed down from the prairie schooner to relieve herself in the privacy of the open prairie all around. The stepfather had clucked the team forward what he considered a safe distance, reined in, and proceeded to tell the girl child how much more he admired her than her mamma, as he tore her duds off. But he'd misjudged how far and fast a worried mother could run, even in skirts and high-buttons. So she'd caught up before he'd had his way with her daughter, and in the resultant considerable confusion he'd wound up going over the tailgate. The hysterical gals had driven off without looking back. It was a sticky mess.

Longarm said, "Ladies, what the man done was shameful, and I'd hit him for you if he was within miles. Meanwhile, let's study on this. You left a man stranded on waterless prairie over a day's ride from anywhere. I'd say by now he's had second thoughts. It's up to you, of course, but it seems mighty hard to leave him in such a condition."

The mother gagged. "I never want to see him again!"

"Me neither," the daughter said. "I'll stick him with my knife if ever I lay eyes on him again!"

Longarm shrugged. "Well, if your minds are made up, I have no right to make you go back for him. I see you have transportation. How are you fixed for grub, water, and loose change?"

"I've railroad fare home for us both, if only I could find a railroad!" the woman said.

He didn't want them traveling his way. He had enough on his plate. "All right, I'll tell you what. Head due north. When you see the first Kansas windmill, head for it. Wherever you find yourselves, the folks will doubtless see you get safely back East in exchange for that team and anything else you don't mean to carry on the train." He turned to the girl. "You'd best slip out here and take the reins, sis. I don't think your mother heard me."

She protested, "I'm naked as a jay, mister!"

"Still? Well, here, I'll just hand you the ends and you

hold on till I'm riding off with my back your way. You won't meet anyone for at least the rest of this day. But I'd sure study on putting *something* on, between here and the Kansas line."

She reached out a naked arm for the reins. Longarm gave them to her. "There you go. Now listen tight. All you have to do is make sure the afternoon sun is shining on your left cheek as you just keep driving, see? Stop when it goes down. In the morning, make sure you drive with the shadows to your left. Sooner or later you'll see a windmill either ahead of you or off to one side. Either way, head for it, and you can work out the rest."

She said she understood, so Longarm got down, chased his two ponies together, and mounted up to ride on. He knew better, but he rode due east instead of the way he'd been trending.

He didn't know just how he'd work it when he came upon a disappointed rapist out in the middle of nowhere, but he couldn't leave even such a skunk stranded to die of thirst and exposure.

He rode quite a ways before he saw carrion crows circling something on the ground ahead. He looked back. The prairie schooner was nowhere in sight. He rode closer. Then, when his mount began to shy, he reined in and dismounted, staking the reins.

He walked forward the last hundred yards, stopped, and stared soberly down at the body lying face up in the grass. The man had been about forty. His face and body were covered with ants. Longarm rolled him over with his boot. The back of his head was caved in.

Longarm walked back to his ponies and took the hatchet from the packsaddle. *Old son, you'd best bury the son of a bitch before some distant riders get to wondering about them crow birds above.*

He knew that technically he was aiding and abetting. But, hell, killing a worthless husband wasn't a federal crime —and shouldn't be. The poor gals deserved a second chance, and likely they didn't even know they'd done the rascal in. It looked like one or the other had hit him harder with a skillet or some such than she might have intended. Longarm saw no need to pester anyone else about it. He was paid to keep the peace, not to pick nits. This no-good bastard was going to be peaceable as hell, from now on.

Chapter 11

Nothing else interesting happened as Longarm rode on to Hitchland. The ride was long and tedious. He could tell, long before he got to the Texas line, that he was coming to the bottom line of No Man's Land. The grassy prairie started turning into the scrubby semi-desert that gave away overgrazing, again.

He rode through it cursing as dry twigs tore at his denim-clad legs, until he came upon a railroad line running northeast to southwest. His map told him it had to be the Rock Island Pacific, so he followed the tracks south, noting that he'd almost overshot.

About five in the afternoon he spied smoke on the horizon ahead. A little while later he could see a dotted line of windmills and tank towers. The sun was setting as he rode into the little jerkwater Texas town of Hitchland.

As he'd assumed, Hitchland was little more than a flag

stop for the railroad. There were some loading pens along the tracks. He'd thought the rebellious Richardsons had gone a mite out of their way to ship Texas beef. On the other hand, the brighter side was that they were almost smack on the line. If the law here was corrupt, stolen cows would be safe to load here.

There was one rinky-dink saloon calling out to the gathering dusk with a not-too-bad piano. Longarm reined in in front of it and got down to tether his brutes. A man with a copper star on his vest and a beat-up old Ranger hat on his head materialized from the shadows of the saloon's overhang and said, "Howdy, stranger."

"Howdy yourself, Constable," Longarm said. "I was meaning to look you up as soon as I inhaled some beer after my long ride. I'm glad to see the law is took so serious here."

"Just doing my job, stranger."

"That's what I just said. I ain't a stranger—I'm the law, too. My name is Custis Long. I'm a deputy U. S. marshal and I was sent down here from Denver to meet up with you, I reckon."

The older town law spat. "Let's see some I.D. afore you tells me what in thunder a Colorado rider's doing here in Texas. It ain't like we don't have a federal marshal in Amarillo, you know."

Longarm said that was a fair request and flashed his badge as he brought the older man up-to-date on his mission. By the time he'd finished, he'd learned to call the lawman Weddington—Pop Weddington. It could have been worse. Half the lawmen down here seemed to want to be called Tex.

Pop Weddington spat again and said, "I know about Latimer. Heard about you, too, Longarm. Heard you don't get along with Texas Rangers. My sister's oldest boy's a Ranger."

"I don't have no kids in the Rangers," Longarm said. "Can't say I ever had harsh words with a Ranger named Weddington, either."

"His last name's Taylor. My sister never had him outten wedlock, damn it."

Longarm smiled and said, "I still disremember biting your nephew on the leg, Pop. I get along with *some* Rangers. Let's talk about Latimer. You want to do it inside, over a beer? I can't spend much time in there. Got to put my ponies up for the night soon. You got a livery here in town?"

"Across the street, yonder. Why don't you board your hosses and we'll go on down to my office. I got all the information on the accident in my desk drawer."

That sounded fine to Longarm. The older man fell in step beside him and, when they got to the livery, told the colored hostler to run the ponies down, treat 'em right, and charge it to the town. So Longarm knew that Pop Weddington's bark was meaner than his bite.

He followed the older man down the walk to the combined lockup and office. There was nobody in the cages. Pop said there would be, come roundup, most any day now.

He sat at a rolltop, opened a drawer, and took out a manila envelope. "These is the personal effects of the run-over man," he said. "What we found, leastways. Him and his duds was scattered some after the train plowed into him."

He emptied the contents on the desk for Longarm's inspection. As Longarm picked up a wallet crusted with dry blood, he asked, "No offense, but didn't it occur to anybody here to let the land office know? I can see by this I.D. card that we're talking about the right Hiram Latimer. It says here in plain English that he's a fee collector for the land office."

Pop Weddington snorted. "Hell, son, give us some credit for being halfways civilized in Texas. Of *course* I sent a letter to the land office. Done so the day after he was kilt by that train. Never got no answer."

"That's odd. They said they had no idea what had happened to him. What did happen to him, by the way?"

"What's left is buried in the churchyard—First Methodist. There was nothing saying if he was Methodist or not, but the Reverend Peabody said he ought to be buried *some*

113

damn decent where. We used some money we found on him to pay for the casket. The rest is still in his wallet."

Longarm noted the two ten-dollar silver certificates and put the wallet down again. He picked up a cheap watch. The hands had stopped at 4:37. The crystal was broken. The older man nodded and said, "That was about the time they must have hit him. The train crew wasn't much help. They said they never noticed running over him out on the prairie."

Longarm turned the watch over, noted Latimer's initials had been inscribed on the back of the case, and asked, "How did they know they run him down, then?"

Pop Weddington gasped. "How did they know? Jesus Christ, boy, I am purely beginning to savvy how you get in so many fights with Rangers! They knew they'd run him down when we *told* them they'd run him down, God blast it! A couple of hands from the Flying M found the scattered remains the next day. Seen carrion crows over above the tracks and suspicioned a Flying M cow might have got hit. They rode in here and told me. Me and the boys rid out with a buckboard. Picked up a leg here and a head there and, like I said, most of what we found is buried over to the First Methodist."

He picked up a jackknife. Its horn handle plate had been broken off one side. Initials had been burned into the other. He said, "We found Latimer's wallet with his I.D. We found his watch and knife with his initials. The head got rolled along the ties some, but folks who knowed him said it sure looked like him. What do you want, a signed statement?"

Longarm took the jackknife. "What happened to his horse? More important, what happened to Latimer's saddlebags? He would have had notebooks, checks, and such in at least one of 'em."

"He couldn't have been riding when he got hit by the train. The crew would have noticed hitting anything that complicated. Give me credit for pondering that point, too. I know it don't make much sense for a man to be wandering afoot on the prairie at four-thirty-seven in the morning. We found him about eight or ten miles out. The train stopped here for water at a quarter to five, so the time his watch stopped fits, give or take a fast watch or a slow train."

Longarm muttered, "Yeah, that was pretty slick, if it was a ruse. Four-forty-three or four would have been suspiciously neat. But we're still missing some pieces, Pop."

"I don't think we left any important parts of him out on the prairie."

"I'm sure you gathered the remains together good. But where the hell was his *horse?*"

Pop Weddington shrugged. "Could have happened a couple of ways. Suppose he fell off, drunk, and the horse run off on him in the dark? He might have been following the tracks back to town, not paying attention as the headlight overtook him."

Longarm put the knife down on the desk. "I'll talk to the railroad crew about that. Sooner or later they have to stop for water here again. I'm still more interested in the missing horse. Latimer was collecting money for Uncle Sam. It's missing, along with his saddlebags and full-grown horse as fit between 'em. Horses have been known to throw a drunken rider, but they don't vanish into thin air after. I've been over the lay of the land to the north. There's nothing to attract a horse out there for at least forty miles. Such oats and water as even a dumb horse would remember are here in Hitchland. I noticed a watering trough just down from the saloon. To save me going back to pester that hostler at the livery, could you tell me if Latimer kept his mount there while in town?"

Pop Weddington nodded. "Sure he did. Where else is there to board a horse while a man's drinking serious? They'll tell you in the saloon that Latimer had an awesome thirst whenever he come in off the range. By the way, one of the barkeeps assisted in the identification of the battered head."

"One middle-aged drunk looks much like any other, Pop. Do you reckon I could get an exhumation order?"

The older man whistled and said, "You sure must have a strong stomach. He's been in the ground a little over two

115

weeks. You'll have to wait till the circuit-riding judge comes by if you want to dig him up lawsome, and I don't know who in hell you'll get to help you. But what in thunder are you being so proddy about, boy? The goddamned body packed Latimer's I.D. The goddamned body was identified by local folks as knowed him when he was alive. And, when Austin gets around to answering the mail, they'll likely identify him as one of their bill collectors, too!"

Longarm blinked. "Austin? You notified the land office in *Austin* about finding Latimer's body?"

"Well, sure I did. That's where the land office *is*, damn it!"

Longarm laughed. "That clears up part of the mystery. Instead of wiring, you sent a poky letter to an office as never *heard* of the poor bastard. Latimer was working out of the *Denver* office! So, assuming your letter's reached Austin, Texas, by now, it's being passed from one desk to another. They won't answer till they make sure someone else down the line might not have heard of a name they can't connect to the nearest water cooler."

Weddington protested, "How the hell was we supposed to know the rascal was connected with Colorado instead of Texas? He was collecting range fees in Texas, damn it! He had no call to be pestering Texas folks for money if he was selling Texas grass and sending the money to Colorado!"

"Now, don't get your bowels in an uproar, Pop. Latimer wasn't selling grazing permits on Texas range. The money from the federal range to the north goes to Washington no matter who collects it. I reckon the No Man's Land strip is managed from Denver. There's surely no town in the strip itself to set up an office in.

"Let's not pick nits. We have enough on our plate without going into government paperwork. Your sending a notification to the wrong office explains how come Denver got so confused about his whereabouts. But it opens up another can of worms on us. The case was brought to the attention of the law when Latimer failed to send money to his family back East. It was his hungry wife and kid who reported him missing in the first place. You say he was killed less than a month ago. His *wife* ain't heard from him for over *eight weeks,* and she's mad as hell about it. You see how the *timing's* sort of messed up?"

Weddington shrugged. "No, I don't. The gent just never got around to writing home. Happens all the time. He wasn't missing when she reported him missing. It was just that he really got kilt about the time everyone *else* started wondering about him."

Longarm shook his head and said, "Latimer didn't send money for his kid personal. He'd made an agreement with the courts to have a part of his pay set aside every month. Like other government employees, he had to sign a voucher ahead of payday every month. Had he done so, the wife and kid would have got their money and never bitched at all."

Weddington frowned. "You mean he missed signing the *pay book* last month?"

"And the month before, it seems. I talked to a gal in his office up Denver ways. She said he was mighty casual about coming in from the field. But even gents who live more sober lives seldom let pay pile up for two months. I got to wire his office about that. Is there a Western Union here in Hitchland?"

"Sure. Over by the depot."

Longarm told Weddington to keep Latimer's effects for now and headed for the door. The old man came with him, damn his nosy soul. Longarm also had some private wires of inquiry to send. He didn't know a polite way to check out the record of a small-town lawman with the rascal reading over his shoulder. But, meanwhile, he could tell Billy Vail he was still alive and where he was. Maybe Waterford, Latimer's boss, could explain why the books were kept so casually at the Denver land office, too.

When they got to the Western Union, the older lawman solved part of Longarm's problem by saying, "You go on in and send your wires, son. I got to spring a leak. I'll mosey around to the alley and wait for you out here."

Longarm nodded, went in, and told the night clerk he had some collect night letters to send. The clerk shoved a pad and pencil his way. The deputy got the message to Billy Vail out of the way first, since he didn't know when the town law might or might not join him, and he wanted Vail to check Weddington out. It was a caution how many re-formed holdup men turned small-town law in their declining years.

He handed the clerk that page and wrote a shorter message to Latimer's boss, wording it politely as he asked how come nobody had wondered why he'd been so casual about coming by to get paid once in a damned while. He sent an even politer message to the Bureau of Land Management in Washington, asking if they had any details on anyone connected with the case that one or more might have skimmed over in passing. He addressed it to a land-office gent he knew personally, who owed his promotion in part to another old land-fraud case Longarm had worked on. There had been a lot of that going around when the Hayes reform administration first took over from old U. S. Grant and his drinking buddies.

He stepped outside and looked around in the gloom for old Pop Weddington. A shot rang out. Longarm was crab-bing to one side and slapping leather when the second one smashed the window behind where he'd just been.

Longarm dropped to one knee behind the watering trough in front of the Western Union office as he fired in the general direction of the last muzzle flash. The buildings across the street were blacked out and he couldn't see worth a damn. Another gun muzzle blossomed orange against black, spat-tering Longarm with tepid water as he returned the com-pliment and moved back the other way just in time. Then another gun flamed far to the south of the one he'd last fired at, and smashed hot lead into the wall of the telegraph office. Two more shots rang out without Longarm being able to see the flashes. Longarm frowned, staying where he was as he held his fire. Off to his right he heard Pop Wedding-ton's voice.

"I got one on the ground, son. How about you?" the lawman called out.

Longarm waited, saw that nobody was shooting at the sound of Pop's voice, and called back, "I don't know if I hit anything or not. Where the hell are you, Pop?"

"Down here—alley entrance. Just coming around from pissing when I saw someone outlined agin the saloon lights down the street, with his gun trained your way."

A cautious voice called out through the shattered window of the Western Union. "Hey, what in hell's going on?"

Longarm said, "We're still working on it. You got an oil lamp in there?"

"I have. But it damn near lost its shade just now. Someone just peppered hell outten my back wall!"

"Don't take it personal. They were after me. Throw the lamp out, and let's see if we can have some light on the subject."

"Do what? This lamp's company property!"

"I'll buy you a new one. *Do* it, damn your eyes!"

There was a moment's hesitation, then an oil lamp sailed out the door to crash and explode in a pool of flaming oil in the street. Neither Longarm nor the older lawman hiding down at the corner of the building were dumb enough to break cover as they stared out at two bodies lying in the dust. But, as others were coming from both directions, attracted by the commotion, and nobody seemed to be shooting at anyone, Longarm stepped down off the walk and strode over to the nearest cadaver, his gun still out just in case.

The man one or the other of them had hulled through the chest was on his back, eyes open and already glazed from staring the dark angel in the face. Old Pop Weddington rolled the other one over with his boot and said, "This one's a candidate for a coffin—whoever the hell he was. What you got over there, Longarm?"

Longarm answered, "Can't say. Never laid eyes on him before." He dropped to one knee, patting down the dead man with his free hand. Pop Weddington joined him to shoo the growing crowd back. "What's the matter with you boys? Ain't you never seen a corpse afore?" the town lawman asked.

Longarm removed a wallet from the cadaver and stood up. "Let 'em look, Pop. Any of you gents ever see this rascal before?"

One of the townsmen said, "I have. Don't know his name, but he's been hanging about the saloon for a few days."

Longarm led the talkative man over to the other corpse, a younger man dressed all in black. The man said, "*Him*, too! They was together. They've both been in town a few days, like they was *waiting* for something."

Pop Weddington snorted. "I sure could offer an educated guess as to who they was waiting for, Longarm. I mind talking to both of them when they rode in two days ago. It's my job to do so. They said they was waiting for a gal who was coming down on the Rock Island Pacific. Don't slight me for buying that, damn it. I kept an eye on 'em, and they seemed to be behaving themselves in my town."

A buck-toothed youth with a faint family resemblance to old Weddington elbowed through the crowd, displaying another mail-order badge pinned to his vest. "I come running as soon as I heard, Pop," he said. "Jesus Christ, who stopped the clocks of these galoots?"

Longarm said, "Pop did, Deputy. He sure shoots good in the dark, and it's getting dark some more as that oil burns away. It's your move, old timer. I ain't the town law."

Pop Weddington nodded and told his deputy, "Get some of the boys and carry these rascals over to the funeral home. We'll figure what to do with 'em, later. I sure feel like having that drink now, Longarm."

Longarm said he did, too, so they headed for the saloon, with half the town following.

The old man was silent until he and Longarm were seated at a corner table alone with tall schooners of needled beer between them. Since he was on an expense account, Longarm's was needled with Maryland rye. He didn't want to do any serious drinking, but he figured he deserved some of the finer things of life after all that excitement.

"I thank you kindly for putting all the blame on me, Longarm," Pop Weddington said. "Was you trying to build my rep, or did you just aim to get out of discussing the matter with the coroner's jury?"

Longarm said, "Both. Coroner's juries tend to spend a lot more time pestering a stranger than they would their own town law. As to making you look good, it's becoming clearer to me by the minute that you *are* pretty good. You wore that hat when you were a Ranger, right?"

The old man shrugged modestly. "I'm retired from the Rangers, but a man likes to keep his hand in. The pension ain't much, the way prices has riz of late. I remember when beer was two cents, and now it's a whole nickel. Goddamn prices are mighty hard on old folks on a fixed income."

Longarm nodded and took a sip of his spiked drink. Pop Weddington had let him have the seat with its back to the wall so Longarm could see everyone in the crowded saloon. Most of them were bellied to the bar celebrating the narrow escape of their town law as if it had been something they'd had a lot to do with.

Longarm saw a gent dressed tinhorn, sitting alone in a far corner, dealing three-card monte wistfully.

"There's a professional card sharp behind you, Pop," Longarm said. "I take it he's made the usual arrangements with the township?"

"That'd be Doc Piper. He's all right. Works the trains. He just stops off here from time to time because Hitchland is the end of the section. Train crews and regular card-playing passengers lay over here to catch the next train north. I've warned Doc not to skin anyone I know. That's why he's alone so much. Why do you ask? He wasn't with them other two. I'd have been told. The barkeeps has standing instructions to tell me if the rascal so much as buys a drink for any of the folks under my personal protection."

121

Longarm nodded. "I said you seemed to know your job. Would that gambling man have been aboard the train that ran Latimer down that night?"

"Sure. He works that section of the line. But what of it? He was playing cards with greenhorns in one of the coaches as they passed over Latimer in the dark. If the engine crew never noticed, how the hell could Doc have?"

Longarm shrugged, took another sip of beer, then lit a smoke to keep from swilling too much too fast. "Which one of the barkeeps identified the body?" he asked. "The tall one or the short, fat one?"

"Short, fat one. Name's Malone. You want to talk to him?"

"Not just yet. I know what he'd say. They get quite a crowd in here for such a one-horse town."

"Well, roundup's coming. Some of them gents are extra pokes for the cattle pens. Others come drifting in this time of summer hoping to sign on as riders. Most spreads need extra help during roundups. The ramrods and even some of the owners come into Hitchland to shop. Meeting up with 'em here beats riding all over creation asking for work."

Longarm said he understood. The fat barkeep was used to serving a transient trade. On the other hand, Latimer had passed through here fairly regularly. Malone would know better than a federal man who'd never seen Latimer if he was the one they'd buried or not. Longarm put that aside for now. He'd dug some bodies up in his time. There had to be a nicer way.

A pretty but painted red-headed gal in a shamefully short, frilly dress that matched her henna rinse came out from a room in back and ignored the round of cheers as she sat down at the upright piano against the wall Longarm had his back to. She started to tickle the ivories pretty decently.

He knew she was the one he'd heard playing the piano earlier. Her profile was to him as she played on, ignoring the crowd. She profiled nice, and her face wasn't bad, either. Pop Weddington followed his gaze and said, "That's

122

Miss Red Robin. She don't put out. Just plays that infernal piano like she's mad at it. Don't know why she's so sulky, but I can't arrest a gal for being unfriendly."

Longarm said that was a shame. "If she plays here regular, she might have noticed the two strangers you just shot," he commented.

"Doubt she paid 'em much mind. As you'll see when she takes her next break, Red Robin don't look at hardly anybody. She just gets up and flounces out with her back to the crowd. Never seen such a stuck-up saloon gal as Red Robin."

"Some saloon gals don't like to hear glass breaking. Is she the private property of somebody given to displays of temper, Pop?"

The older man shook his head and said, "It's my understanding she sleeps alone. I know the owner of this joint personal, so I can tell you *he* ain't getting any of it. She has a room upstairs. That's where she hangs out betwixt fits of piano-busting. She only works twelve hours a day, from noon to midnight. Her morning are free, but you know how women can be in small trail towns, so I don't reckon she had any she-male pals, neither."

Longarm stared thoughtfully at the pretty piano player. She was aware of it and her cheeks grew red. But she didn't look his way as she went on hammering out "Up In a Balloon" as if it were a quick march. She hit all the notes right, but a sensitive cuss could see she'd rather be up in that infernal balloon right now than where she was. Longarm couldn't think of any way to assure her that his interest was purely professional without likely convincing her it wasn't, so he looked away.

"Speaking of private rooms, Pop," he said, "I've been bedding down on dry grass and hard ground of late, and I'd sure like a night's rest in a real bed. A place with a bath within walking distance would be even better. Is there a hotel in town?"

Weddington shook his head. "Nope. Some takes in boarders, but at this time of the year you'll find most of the rooms for hire already booked. I'd put you up at my place, but me and the old woman only has one bed, and, no offense, I prefers my wife to sleep with me."

"I can see I'll wind up in the livery hayloft, then."

The older man said, "You'd best get cracking, then. Half the saddle tramps who board their ponies there likely have their bedrolls already spread on all the soft spots above the stalls."

Longarm grimaced and took another swig of needled beer. "Oh, well, I reckon I can find at least one patch of grass to spread my sleeping bag on on your overgrazed range to the north. But I sure am starting to find it tedious. Once you've seen one shooting star, you've seen 'em all."

"Hold on," the old man said. "I might be able to work something out with the gent who owns this saloon. He don't live here. He's got more sense. But, like I said, he's got rooms upstairs. Place used to be a whorehouse, afore the last owner lost his license. The cribs is decent now. Mayhaps a mite dusty, but the beds is still there. There's a bath and a flush commode at the end of the hall, too. Let's go see if he'll give you a key."

Longarm said, "We'd save me some time if you was to be neighborly enough to work it out without me, Pop. It's early yet. I mean to talk with folks before they all bed down. What say I meet you here about . . . when's your bedtime?"

"You name the time and this is the place. My old woman don't expect it every night from a man my age, and I'll never get to sleep, wondering what you've been up to. Who are you fixing to talk to, that barkeep?"

"Later, maybe, when things quiet down in here near closing time. I thought the undertaker would be as good a place to start as any. How do I find the rascal?"

"Just down the street, past that telegraph office. He keeps a light in his front glass. The tricky part is that it's a hardware store between funerals. Sad Sam Dillon just buries folk as a sideline. He makes the coffins in the back as a way to

pass the time. He don't sell all that much lumber and hardware, neither."

Longarm thanked the lawman for the directions, said he'd
be back by eleven-thirty, and left. The piano was playing
"Old Folks At Home," as if the old folks were running like
hell.

Chapter 12

Longarm could hear the piano way down the street in the darkness as he walked away. Red Robin sure had strong fingers for a gal. He saw some townsfolk up ahead, staring into the illuminated front glass of a shop. As he joined them, he saw what they were staring at. The two gunslicks he'd shot it out with earlier were on public display, propped up in the window on planks. According to the suspiciously new I.D. papers they'd been carrying, one had been named Johnson and the other Smith. It was small wonder Sad Sam Dillon was hoping someone would come forward to claim them. Small towns didn't pay much for unclaimed stiffs to be disposed of.

The automatic bell over the door brought a tall, raw-boned gent out from the back as Longarm entered. Aside from the two dead men in the front window, the interior of the establishment looked much like any other hardware store. Sad Sam Dillon looked hopeful until Longarm told him who he was. Then the undertaker muttered, "Shit, I already heard who gunned 'em. I was hoping you could tell me who to send the *bill* to! You know I barely breaks even on what this infernal town pays for burials?"

"I'll send out a description on 'em by wire come morning, when someone who might want them might be awake. I figure they were riding under made-up names, and they describe sort of commonplace."

"One has a tattoo. The older one had a dagger and a scroll reading 'Death Before Dishonor' on his right forearm. I noticed it as I was embalming."

"You embalmed 'em both?" Longarm asked.

"Had to. It's a warm night. I'll tell you a secret about their clothes, if that's what you're wondering about. I slit ever'thing but their boots up the back. Didn't have to take their boots off to shoot 'em full of formaldehyde. You want to see my embalming works? I got it in the cellar. Ever'thing's up to date, just like a full-time funeral parlor. I studied it in Chicago, come out West to bury folk full time. How was I to know them Wild West magazines had it wilder than it really was? Sometimes I can go months without getting to bury nobody, damn it."

Longarm nodded and said, "It do seem a peaceable little town, up until recent. I wanted to talk to you about your services for the late Hiram Latimer. I understand he was messed up pretty bad."

"That's for damned sure," Dillon said. "Don't never get run over by a train if you want an open-casket service, Deputy Long. I done the best I could. I pickled all the pieces and laid 'em more or less in place in the coffin. Had to bury him nekked, of course. His clothes was tore up too, and it seemed a waste of time to launder and sew 'em back together, so..."

"What did you do with his duds?" Longarm asked.

The undertaker thought, shrugged, and said, "Throwed 'em in the trash bin out back. Why? Surely you don't have no *use* for bloody rags, do you?"

"I might. Has anyone carried off your trash since it happened?"

"Hell, *sure* they has! Hitchland ain't uncivilized enough to let trash pile up for weeks."

"I said it seemed a nice little town. Where does it get rid of its trash, Sad Sam?"

"Town trash dump, of course. It's about a mile out to the east, downwind, behind a hill of coal ash the railroad dumps as well when they cleans the fireboxes over to the railroad yards. You'll never find old Latimer's duds over there. By now they've been covered with two weeks' leavings from the whole damn town!"

Longarm took out a notebook and pencil stub. "Maybe after sunrise, when a man can see what he's poking about in. Tell me what the dead man was wearing when he got hit by that train."

Sad Sam pursed his lips. "Let's see, now. I turned the contents of his pockets over to old Pop. He was wearing low-heeled stovepipe boots; checkered wool pants; blue flannel shirt—mayhaps army surplus; leather vest—greasy, even before he bled all over it. Oh, yeah, he had a red print bandanna in his hip pocket, not about his neck, which was just as well, considering a rail flange run right over his Adam's apple and took his head off clean. They found his hat a ways down the track. Stetson, pearl gray, when he bought it, but rained-on an' sun-bleached to a sort of cobweb-uninteresting. That's about it."

"No underwear?"

"Nope. Old drunks hardly ever keep underwear on after they shit their britches a time or two. I could see he was a drunk long before anyone told me. Had one of them drinker's noses, all red and rough. Since he was cut up anyways, I took a professional look at his liver. If the train hadn't done him, that pickled liver would have, most any time."

"Did you ever meet Hiram Latimer alive?" Longarm asked.

"Sure. Seen him around town, leastways. He never come in to buy hardware or bury a relation. I knew he was the land agent. Boys pointed him out, sort of cussing. Cowmen sure hate to pay for grass. Mayhaps that was why he drunk

128

alone. Even if he'd been a less worthless-looking cuss, he wouldn't have been popular, taxing Texas men for range they'd been reared to consider free."

Longarm put his notebook away and asked if he could buy a coal-oil lamp. Sad Sam was proud to sell him one, but a bit put off when Longarm said to charge it to his office.

Longarm carried the new lamp back to the Western Union, handed it over, and told the night man he wanted to send some more telegrams. He asked Billy Vail to scout up a better description, mentioning the details of Latimer's last wardrobe.

He asked a few more questions less important and, since it was a night letter, brought Billy up to date on what he'd found so far. It was none of his business whether Latimer's widow got his piled-up paychecks or not, so he didn't suggest it.

But as he left the Western Union a second time he couldn't help wondering why a man who couldn't afford clean underwear hadn't seen fit to report in to get paid for at least two months. It would have made sense if Latimer had been killed that far back. But the undertaker would have noticed if anyone had tried to palm off a six- or eight-week-old corpse on him as a recent accident. A cadaver could stay reasonably fresh on ice for that long, but it wouldn't bleed all over the place when it was cut up by train wheels.

Thinking of train wheels made Longarm head over to the railroad yards. There was no train in sight, of course, and the dispatcher he found in the shed near the roundhouse said there wasn't one due before midnight, if he wanted to go north. Longarm said, "I wanted to jaw some with you about that accident just up the tracks."

The railroad man grimaced. "I figured you might. The insurance dicks have been pestering the hell out of us about it. I told 'em I was right here at the time and that it's no business of mine whether an engineer and fireman are good pals or not."

"Run that by me again. Is the Rock Island Pacific suspicious something naughty might have been going on aboard its locomotive when it hit that gent on the tracks?"

The dispatcher shrugged and said, "It's company regulations to have someone sort of watching the tracks as the engine's moving full steam. The grade was dead flat, the headlamp was shining down the tracks at least a quarter of a mile. A man ain't as big as a cow, but since cows wander onto the tracks all the time at night, they should have been watching."

Longarm nodded. "It struck me the same way—no offense. Is the same crew working this section tonight?"

"Brakemen and such, but not the engine crew. They both got fired when they couldn't account for their actions."

Longarm took out his notebook and recorded both their names before asking the dispatcher where they might be now, and just what the railroad suspected them of. The dispatcher said, "If they never seen him till too late, it was reckless railroading. If they ran over him deliberate, it was worse." He added, "Engineer went east to the Missouri line. Sissy brakeman was last seen riding the rails west. I issued him a pass to get him the hell out of my section. Don't know where he got off, and don't care."

"How come you call him a sissy?" Longarm asked. "Didn't he shovel coal good? They say that train was moving under a full head of steam when it hit old Latimer."

The dispatcher grinned sort of dirty and said, "He had other sissy habits when the firebox was full. I'll deny this if you repeat it, but since the insurance men figured it, I may as well tell the law. The fireman was a queer. Engineer was just a horny rascal. A man gets bored on a long prairie run."

Longarm frowned. "Them's mighty serious charges, pard. Leaving aside they were supposed to be watching the track, a man can do twenty at hard for getting caught at that in some states."

"Hell, who's likely to catch a fireman going down on a man in the privacy of a locomotive cabin in the middle of nowheres? The way the insurance dicks figured it, the horny old engineer had his hand on the throttle, but was gazing down fondly at the top of the fireman's head when it happened. As to how serious the charge might or might not be, you can ask about the roundhouse if you don't believe me. That sissy fireman asked more than one yard man here if he wanted a suck. Nobody took him up on it that I know of. Despite his other disgusting habits, he was too big to hit unless he got persistent, and he was too slick to do that. I reckon he had more time to talk his engine driver into it, since they rode alone together so often."

Longarm grimaced. "Well, I can see why they got fired, whether the tale is true or not. How did they take it when you told them why they didn't work for the Rock Island Pacific no more?"

"They both denied it, of course. Would *you* admit you run over a man whilst enjoying a blow job? The engineer said, private, that he knowed his fireman was sort of strange, but that he himself had a steady gal up at the north end of the section."

"Did he?"

"Sure. Everyone knowed he was shacked up with a Cherokee gal betwixt runs. But lots of gents who has a wife and kids enjoy variety from time to time, and, like I said, that fireman was mighty willing."

"Did the engineer file an official accident report?"

"He did. It's at company headquarters, so I can't show you a copy, but it's easy to remember. He said he was at the throttle staring down the track for cows, and never noticed he'd run over anyone till he heard of it later. He allowed he might have missed something low on the tracks, being it was near the end of a long, tedious run and he was sort of tired of looking at nothing much. He bitched about the cow catcher, too."

"Come again with cow catchers?"

"Hell, ever'body knows what's a cow catcher. They got one in front of ever' locomotive. The idea is to shunt cows outten the way instead of rolling over them and maybe derailing. The insurance men agreed a cow couldn't have

131

fit under the bottom of the cow catcher that night, but a man's a lot skinnier than a cow. They figure the reason the body was torn up so was that the cow catcher did hit him, tossed him ass-over-teakettle down the tracks, and then the train run over him as he was laying there. The engineer said he had to have been laying there ahead of time, but that don't work. Why in thunder would anyone be laying on the track at four-thirty-seven in the morning?"

Longarm didn't know, either. Dillon would have noticed if there'd been any bullets in the body, for he'd cleaned and embalmed all the pieces. It was possible Latimer had simply been so dead drunk he had just passed out on the tracks as he was walking them back to town. Longarm put his note-book away and left after thanking the dispatcher. He walked back slowly to the saloon, sorting his thoughts.

On the one hand, it seemed open and shut that there was no mystery at all here. Standing or lying, a known drunk had been run down by a train. Whether the engine crew was watching the tracks or not, they couldn't have planned to run over a man who was free to step aside when he saw the headlight coming across open prairie at him from miles away. So chasing the train crew down was likely a waste of time. The only charge he had against either was pure carelessness, or sexual preferences that were none of a deputy marshal's business.

He decided to let the Rock Island Pacific off for now. They hadn't killed Latimer out of personal spite. But he couldn't see how anyone else might have, either. Sure, someone could leave a drunk on a railroad track. But then what? They'd have no way of knowing whether the train crew would be keeping a sharp eye out or not. Aside from a train stopping in time, there were other things that could go wrong. You just never knew when the drunkest cuss on earth was suddenly going to rise up. Rolling a yard or so either way would have saved Latimer. It was a careless way to murder a gent, and somebody slicker had been trying to murder Longarm himself ever since he'd been on the case.

He lit a cheroot and mused. *There's the kicker, old son.*

If you got rid of a gent you didn't like by leaving him on a railroad track, and the law put it down to misadventure, why the hell would you be trying to gun a lawman, instead of just letting him write it off as an accident?

Somebody didn't want Longarm to find something out. But what could that something be? That Latimer was dead?

Hell, everybody agreed Latimer was dead. Nobody had tried to gun the lawmen who'd found him or the undertaker who'd buried him. Nobody pestered the witnesses who'd come forward to identify the body either. Was it to keep him from looking at said body? He didn't know what Latimer looked like!

He snapped his fingers, went back to the Western Union, and took out his notebook once more. He found Latimer's home address back East and wired the local police. He left it up to them how they got hold of an old photograph to send him. If the skunk had been married, there should be at least some wedding photos, and the plates might still be at the local photograph studio.

As he handed the blank over, the clerk said he sure was having a busy night. Longarm nodded and said, "Yeah. By the way, did either of them rascals as busted your other lamp ever come in here to send or pick up messages?"

"Not whilst I was on duty," the clerk said. "I'll ask the day man when he relieves me. By then he'll have seen the stiffs in Dillon's hardware."

Longarm thanked him and went back to the saloon. Red Robin was still beating hell out of her piano. He'd never heard "Old Black Joe" played so fast.

Longarm bellied up to the bar, looking in the mirror behind it for Pop Weddington. The town law hadn't come back yet. It wasn't time. As luck would have it, he was served by short, fat Malone. He introduced himself and questioned Malone about the dead man found up the line. The barkeep didn't tell him anything new. He'd served many a drink to the face attached to the severed head they'd shown him, and that was all.

Longarm had some Maryland rye neat, and then Pop

Weddington came in, handed him a key, and said, "It's all fixed up. You just go on up and hit the sack any time you've a mind to. Did you find out anything?"

"No, and I'm sore as hell about that, too. I'll tell you true that if a mess of hired guns hadn't worked so hard to keep me from coming down here, I'd be leaving now, satisfied. But as it is, come morning, I have to keep digging. All the cow spreads either way run cows on the open range to the north, right?"

"Sure—didn't you say it was overgrazed? I see your plan. You mean to find out who paid what, and how much Latimer had in them saddlebags as was never found."

"You're right, Pop. Is there anything I should know about the tender dispositions of people on the spreads up and down the line?"

"You mean serious dispositons as could get a man gunned? I can't say they're likely to butcher the fatted calf for you at every spread you visit. But I doubt anyone will gun a man with your reputation just for practice. Old Latimer was pestering 'em regular and they never gunned him."

"I don't know that for certain. I'll take your word anyone ornery is too sneaky for open warfare."

"Yeah, I've been studying on that missing horse with his saddlebags aboard. He was riding a chestnut gelding with one white stocking, off hind leg, branded with two oxbows."

"I know the brand. It fits. The double oxbow's a Colorado stud farm near Denver. I already knew he road off on a Colorado horse. But I'll keep an eye peeled for it. Thanks, Pop."

The old man said he was welcome and added that if he didn't need him for anything else, it had been a long day, so they shook hands and parted friendly.

Longarm had one last drink for the stairs and went up to find his flop. He struck a light in the long, dark hallway upstairs. He tried the first door, but saw he'd made a mistake. The one-time crib had been fixed up with lace curtains and such, and a stuffed doll stared at him down the length

134

of a bed covered with henna-red quilting. He backed out. He could still hear Red Robin pounding the keyboard downstairs, so no harm had been done.

He struck another light and found that the next room was occupied only by a narrow bed with the mattress rolled up. He lit a wall lamp and rolled the mattress down. Bedding was wadded up inside it.

Hoping it had been laundered at least once since this had been a whorehouse, Longarm shook out the sheets and pillowcases and saw that they were only a mite musty from time's passage. He made up the bed, took off some of his things, and consulted his watch. Red Robin wouldn't be coming up for a spell. He went out, leaving the door ajar so the light spilled out in the passage, and hunted down the bath at the end of the hall.

He ran the hot-water tap, and while the water came out the color and temperature of horse piss, it would do. He locked the door, stripped, and bathed. As he was finishing, since the tepid water didn't tempt him to linger, he heard the piano downstairs stop, as if someone had pole-axed Red Robin. He climbed out of the tub and dried off in a hurry, knowing she'd likely feel sweaty, too. He heard her footsteps passing as he pulled on his boots and jeans. she even *walked* like she was sore at the world. He strapped on his gun but left his shirt open with the tails hanging out. He'd heard her door slam, hard, and knew she wasn't waiting in the hall to peek at him. She would have seen the light under the bathroom door and, in any case, she had doubtless been told he was up here.

He left the lamp lit in the bathroom and stepped out. The light was on under her door now. He called out, "It's all yours, ma'am. I rinsed the tub, and I hope I left some warm water."

He got no answer, but he hadn't expected to. He walked to the partly open door of the crib he'd picked and stepped inside. Then he stopped and frowned soberly down at the little nickel-plated whore's pistol in Red Robin's hand. "Hell,

I said I rinsed the tub, ma'am," he said.

The redhead snapped, "Don't get funny with me, Long-arm! I know who you are!"

"So do I, ma'am. It's no mystery about me being up here. Didn't they tell you downstairs that the boss said I could bed down here for the night?"

"They did, and in a minute they'll all be gone for the night and we'll be all alone up here."

"I thought I heard shutters being pulled across a window just now. I confess I sure feel silly, Red Robin. I knew they had hired guns out after me, but I never figured on a pretty little redhead getting the drop on me in the end."

She shrugged. "I don't want to kill you," she said sullenly.

"Don't, then," he said. "I sure won't mind. I seem to be missing something here, Red Robin. Would you mind telling me who hired you, seeing as you have me at your mercy?"

She frowned and said, "Hired? Nobody hired me, you fool. Unbuckle that belt, very gently, and let your gun just fall before you step away from it into yon corner."

He sighed and did as she said, asking conversationally, "Have you always been redheaded, ma'am? I sure admire redheads, no matter what color hair they has."

She sighed. "So you *did* know. They told me you were good. I guess I have no choice now. It's you or me, and I swore they'd never take me alive, so . . ."

Longarm moved. His left hand shot out like a sidewinder and he clamped it around the cylinder of her little .32 as she tried to pull the trigger. She pulled good. He'd noticed she had strong fingers. But she didn't have the leverage to pull the double action and revolve the cylinder against his grip.

She raked at his face with her nails and gave a frightened scream as he caught that wrist, too, and simply bulled her backward until they lay atop the bed with her on the bottom. He wrenched the gun from her hand and threw it aside to

136

grab that wrist, too, and flatten both down on the pillow on either side of her red hair as she tried to knee him and spat like a cat.

He wedged a knee between her thighs. He did it to pin her better, but of course she yelled, "If you rape me I'll have the law on you!"

He bounced on her some to shake her sensible as he laughed and said, "We just established that the law's already here, Red Robin. I hardly ever rape she-male prisoners, so quiet down and let's study this situation. Would it help if I was to tell you I don't have a clue as to what in hell you've been talking about?"

"Don't play funny with me, damn it. And get your damned knee out of my crotch! You've turned the tables on me, but I'm not going back to that hellhole. I swear you'll never carry me back there, even chained hand and foot!"

"You'd be surprised how often I've had this same dumb conversation with folks who didn't want to go with me some damn place or another, Red Robin. I confess that most of them have been men, though. I'm going to let go of you now. You just lay right the way you are unless you really want to see some serious law enforcement, hear?"

He rolled off her and sprang lightly to his feet to scoop up all the shooting irons on the floor. She just lay there, shooting daggers with her hazel eyes. She'd drawn her legs up as he rolled off, so he could see that her real hair coloring went with her eyes. She was black-headed between the thighs. Her stockings were black above her high-buttons, too. He put the guns up on a high shelf as far from the bed as possible and turned back to her, smiling thinly as he pondered aloud, "Now let me see. I'm damned if I can remember a federal want out on a hazel-eyed gal with coal-black hair."

She gasped as she followed the line of his admiring eyes and lowered her skirts as she crossed her legs. "You damned old peeping Tom! Isn't any secret safe from you?"

He moved back to sit on the edge of the bed, penning

her politely in it. "I knew downstairs you'd done that hair with bleach and henna, Red Robin," he told her. "You go out of your way to be red, don't you?"

"You can't take me back to prison. Please. I'll do anything, Longarm!"

He didn't answer. He'd already found out she was a brunette who'd busted out of some woman's prison. If he gave her more rope, he might figure out some more without telling her how dumb she was.

"I figured you might be out to tempt a man who wasn't easy to shoot," he said. "I admire the coy way you hoisted your knees just now. It's a pure caution how many she-male suspects try to compromise an arresting officer with that old dodge. The hell of it is, it works more often than it should. But since we're both old pros, you know you can't tempt me that easy, as pretty as I find you."

She moaned in fear and then, slowly and deliberately, spread her knees wide and slid her skirt up around her waist. "Please don't take me back to Illinois. I swear I never meant to shoot him in the thigh. He attacked me, working late at night in the office, and..."

"Now, Red Robin, are you sure you wasn't caught dipping in the office safe after hours by someone you figured had left for the evening? That's another old familiar tale, too, you know."

"That's what the jury believed, but I swear it never happened like that at all! Mr. Chalmers said he wanted me to stay late to work, but he made advances. As we struggled, there was this gun atop the office safe and... he lied at my trial and... oh, God, I'll do anything to keep from going back there! I'll let you lay me! I'll let you put it anywhere you want, darling!"

Longarm sighed, put a hand between her creamy thighs, and said, "This'd do fine, if I was a weak-willed, worthless scamp. You sure are gushing nice for a gal that was just set to volley a mess of .32's into me. Is it passion or just willingness?"

138

She grabbed the back of his hand in both of hers and started jerking off with his fingers. "Both, maybe. I haven't had a man since I escaped from prison. Don't turn me in. I swear I've gone straight and I do so want to be your *friend!*"

"Well, my head knows better, but my pecker has a mind of its own," Longarm said. "So let's get out of these duds and get acquainted."

"You swear you won't arrest me after?"

"Hell, girl, I'd get arrested myself if I tried. You knew before you started seducing me that it's against the rules to make love to a she-male prisoner!"

She laughed with weak relief and proceeded to haul her red dress off as if it were full of red ants.

He shucked almost as fast, and as she started to roll down her black stockings he said, "Leave 'em be. The best parts are on public display, and I sure do admire all I see."

As he moved to mount her, she asked, "Can't we have the lamp out? I suddenly feel so awkward."

"I have to keep my eye on the guns up yonder as well as you, Red Robin," he said. So she lay back and closed her eyes, keeping a stiff upper lip as she resigned herself to her fate. He knew she wasn't offering out of pure affection. But, hell, he didn't like *her* all that much!

As he parted the thick black thatch between her white thighs with his excited shaft, he decided he liked her better.

As she felt it sliding into her she gasped and seemed to think better of him, too, judging by the way she wrapped her arms about him, spread her legs wider, and began to bump and grind with a high heel dug into the mattress on either side of his naked legs.

He didn't expect her to climax with him. He didn't care. A gal who'd just been out to gun him owed him more courtesy than he owed her. So he was surprised, and she was, too, when she suddenly gasped, "Oh, I never expected this, but I fear I'm coming!"

He kissed her to keep her from talking so foolish and as

he exploded inside her he could tell by her contractions and the way she started hammering with her high heels that her natural feelings had overcome her distaste for the law.

They went limp in each other's arms for a spell, enjoying the afterglow as they tongued each other friendly. When they came up for air, Red Robin sighed. "I think I still hate you," she said. "I know I'm trying to. But could we do it at least one more time?"

Longarm laughed, said he was willing to try, and moved them around so her tail lay on the edge of the mattress as he braced his bare feet on the rug. He hooked one of her knees over each of his elbows and opened her wide for serious pounding. Her eyes gaped. "That's too deep," she protested, and "I'm embarrassed to be seen in this position, even by a lover!"

He said, "Don't worry, consider me an *enemy*," as he braced himself on stiff arms to admire himself sliding in and out of her. She started rolling her red hair all over the sheet as she begged him to do it faster. This time she came ahead of him, but not by much. As he went limp and released her legs she wrapped them around his waist and sighed. "Oh, that was lovely," she said. "I hope you're not going to arrest me, now that you'd had your way with me, dear."

He laughed as he moved them both into a more neighborly position on the bed. He held her against him, partly because it felt so good and partly to keep her from acting foolish about the guns on the shelf. "I never meant to arrest you," he said. "What you did wasn't a federal crime in the first place, and I'm on a more important mission, in the second. I reckon I could have turned you over to Texas for pointing guns at a federal agent, and Pop Weddington might have seen fit to see if Illinois still wanted you, or if there's a reward out on you. But, hell, that'd mean filling out all sorts of fool papers. And, like I said, I'm busy."

She started to pull away. She would have, too, if he hadn't been the stronger of them. "Why, you . . . you *bastard!*" she blazed. "You took advantage of a helpless woman!"

"I sure did. And wasn't it fun?"

She laughed despite herself. "You're just awful. I should never speak to you again, but . . . Longarm?"

"Yeah, Red Robin?"

"Could you manage again, if I got on top this time?"

Chapter 13

Longarm got out to the city dump early the next morning after a warm night's sleep and a cool breakfast. The morning was cool, too, but it still smelled awful on the far side of the high ridge of coal ashes.

Everything from busted baby buggies to soggy paper sacks of rotting table scraps lay scattered for a couple of acres in a festering mat at least six feet deep. He stared morosely at a rat nibbling bold as brass almost close enough to kick. "Hell, rat," Longarm told it, "there's no way on earth to find a few shreds of bloody rags in all this shit!"

He sensed movement behind him and turned to see a tall, shabby figure coming his way from what looked like a hobo jungle down at the far end. The hobo was dressed in the seersucker shirt and cap of a railroad crewman. His pants were faded denim. He didn't have any serious hardware strapped around his waist, so Longarm nodded and said,

"Morning. You drop off that train I heard about midnight last night?"

The big man's voice was high and whiny as he replied. "I did. I had to come back and clear my name. What are *you* looking for?"

"The duds that gent you run over was wearing. Are you Hoskins or Green?"

"I'm Sparky Green. What else did they tell you about me?"

"Just that you were the fireman aboard the engine that night. Anything else anyone said is none of my affair. I'm a federal deputy, not a guardian of public morals."

Green's pink lips quivered and he looked like he was fixing to start bawling. "I ain't no damn queer," he said. "That story was started by a roundhouse drunk who really is. I've always had trouble with queers. They just can't understand that some fellers just naturally has high-pitched voices."

Longarm nodded, neither convinced nor concerned about details like that. He kicked an old busted door panel over, noting nothing under it but maggots crawling in damp, stinky stuff with checked wool or blue flannel mixed with it. He said, "This could take a man all day, working with a pitchfork. How were you fixing to clear your name, Sparky Green?"

"Well, first I meant to whup hell outten that roundhouse queer and make him confess I wasn't like *him!* But the son of a bitch had moved up the line."

"I don't think it'd work, no offense. I suspect he was transferred for the same reason you and your engine driver were fired. Insurance dicks are like that. It's their job to confuse the issue, lest relatives of the dear departed start a fearsome lawsuit. But I'll tell you what, Sparky, I know some friendly railroad officials on other lines. I'll pass the word next time I ride the Burlington, that you may have got a raw deal and that the late Hiram Latimer's widow lives way the hell off and likely won't feel like suing once she gets her husband's federal insurance. If I were you, I'd

143

forget it. Even if you could prove you was riding the cow catcher staring down the tracks with a spyglass that night, no insurance dick is ever going to admit a mistake once he's signed his report."

The ex-fireman said, "I *was* looking down the tracks. Me and Hoskins *was* bending the rules a mite that night, but not the way the company thinks. I was at the throttle. That's how a fireman gets to be an engine driver, if he can get a decent cuss to show him the ropes." .

"I savvy the apprentice system. Could you tell me for sure you were wide awake at said throttle at four-thirty-seven that morning?"

"I surely was, for driving a locomotive is interesting as hell when you don't get to *do* it much. Hoskins let me take over out in the middle of that long, straight stretch down through No Man's Land whilst he et and coffeed, setting on the coal. He'd said to look out for cows on the tracks as we approached Hitchland through open range, so I was keeping my eyes peeled all the way."

"And?"

"And nothing. I never run over *nobody!* The night was clear, the tracks was clear, the headlamp had just been cleaned, and it was throwing its beam way down them shiny tracks."

Longarm said, "Well, I wasn't there, and you're too big to call a liar, but the fact remains that *some* damn something run over that gent. There was no other train going either way between the time you boys made the run and some cowboys found him scattered from hell to breakfast along the right of way."

"I've been thinking about that like a puppy chawing a slipper," Green said, "and I come up with a way that works. Suppose he was never walking or laying on the tracks ahead of us? Suppose he fell between the cars in *back* of us? If Latimer was aboard the train as a passenger, got drunk and missed his step as he wandered from car to car..."

Longarm shook his head. "There's a hole in it, Sparky. You were coming down from the north line of the strip.

144

There ain't a stop where the victim could have boarded the train that night for over forty or fifty miles from here, where he'd just been seen hanging about the saloon."

Sparky Green looked like a man who'd spent ten dollars on a gal and didn't get to kiss her good night. "Well, damn it," he blurted, "couldn't he have got fifty miles up the track some damn way, boarded our combo, and fell between cars, like I said?"

Longarm started to object. Then he frowned and said, "Hmm, we do seem to be missing a horse. But that's a mighty serious ride, drunk or sober. And why in hell would a man ride north that far just to get on a train to Hitchland, when he was already here to begin with?"

"Mayhaps he forgot something he had to come back for. Look, if a man druv his horse into the ground on a long hard ride and had to go back in a hell of a hurry, couldn't he have boarded a train to do so?"

Longarm shrugged. "There's all sorts of could-be notions, and just-possibles, Sparky. I like to work with most-likelys. But I'll keep your complicated timetable in mind as I poke about for more sensible explanations."

He reached in his pocket, took out his wallet, and handed the down-at-the-heels gent a one-dollar note, saying, "Here, I've been there, too. If I was standing in your shoes, I'd hop me the next train out. I buy most of your tale, but you'll play hell getting a job in *this* town, anyways. I got to move it on, Sparky. So good luck and good morning to you."

He left the dump. He hadn't found what he'd hoped to. He wasn't sure he'd learned anything from the ex-fireman, either. It was a caution how folks lied to the law. Even if Sparky had been leveling with him, it just served to mix him up even more.

Longarm went to the telegraph office, picked up a couple of wires, and put them away to read when he got the time. He went to the livery, got old Paint, and rode out to the west. As time passed he started seeing cows and windmills. He'd never had a serious conversation with a cow, so he headed for a windmill. When he reined in at the soddy under it, a bitter-faced old gent came out and said he was trespassing. Longarm said he was doing no such thing, and flashed his badge. So the stockman said in that case he'd talk to him.

He didn't have much to say. He complained about the summer being so dry and the range so poor just as the price of beef was rising. "I lost a mess of calves this summer," he said. "Their mammas can't keep milk in their udders, browsing on dry chaparral."

"How many head are you raising on this quarter section, pard?"

"Eight hundred, last tally. Likely fewer, next. Naturally, most of 'em graze on the open range to the north. But you can see from here it's gone to brush as fur as the eye can see."

Longarm nodded. "That's one of the things I wanted to ask you about. Did you buy a grazing permit from Hiram Latimer a short time back, and can I see it?"

"I did and you can," said the bitter-faced man, reaching in his hip pocket. He handed up a folded, greasy slip of paper.

Longarm unfolded it, saw it was a standard form, and handed it back. "Says on your permit that you only hired grass for four hundred head," he said.

"Does it? Well, maybe I miscounted some. I don't know why I bragged on eight hundred just now. It's come back to me I sold half the herd a spell back, and it likely slipped my mind."

Longarm said that was reasonable and rode on. By the time he'd visited a couple more spreads, a new pattern was emerging, and the late Hiram Latimer figured to get fired—whether he was in the churchyard or not. For the stupid son of a bitch had been selling Uncle Sam's grass at a loss.

Most of the people he talked to were too smart to admit they ran more cows on federal land than their permits allowed, but Longarm knew which end of a cow the bullshit came out of. It was easy to judge from the look of an outfit and the condition of the surrounding prairie when they forgot

146

to mention five to six hundred extra head. One sweet-look-ing little old lady in a sunbonnet told him that she and her husband only kept fifty head or so, but she had two daisy windmills pumping water enough for a couple of fair-sized stockyards. He didn't ask if they'd bribed Latimer or just thought he was in need of specs. Either answer could be true, and people hardly ever told family secrets to passing strangers, badge or no.

He rode on, taking out the telegrams and scanning them to pass the time. Billy Vail had talked to Latimer's boss, so one question was answered. Mr. Waterford *had* decided to fire Latimer when and if he ever showed up, but hadn't reported him missing for two reasons. He'd suspected La-timer was off on another drunken toot and hadn't been all that worried about him. And he'd covered for him on past occasions and seemed to be one of those office politicians who neither liked to rock the boat nor admit mistakes to the higher-ups. He'd just set Latimer's back pay aside—on the books, not in cash. He hadn't sent anything to Latimer's wife and child because he couldn't until Latimer signed for his paychecks. He had a fair-sized payroll and most of it made sense, so he didn't read the fine print on vouchers nobody came in to collect on.

The land office sure has a mess of sloppy thinkers working for it, old son, Longarm mused. *Of course, old Waterford's up in Denver. So you can't blame him for the way this range looks, thanks to that shiftless Latimer. Hope it was him the train run over, for it's going to take years for the range to recover from his neglectful ways.*

That reminded him of the only reason he had for sus-pecting there was more to this case than a dumb old drunk getting killed by accident. But when he looked back, nobody was trailing him.

He spied a windmill ahead. He saw as he rode closer that something odd was happening. The brush to the north started giving way to grass. It was overgrazed some, stripped bare in spots, and you couldn't say the range was being cared for as a front lawn might have been. But at least the folks at the next spread seemed to be using common sense instead of naked greed. He saw a quartet of cows off to the north, just outside rifle range. One had a calf, half-grown and healthy looking, grazing at her side. The cows were at least part white-face, too.

As he rode into the spread, he saw that the soddy had been whitewashed and there were checked curtains in the windows. A couple sat side by side on the veranda as he rode up and reined in. The husband stood up and howdied Longarm as the wife went inside to put on the coffee.

As Longarm dismounted, he saw that the gent was older than him, but still spry and lean from riding. They shook hands as Longarm introduced himself. The man said they could coffee inside or out on the veranda. Longarm said it was warming up for setting inside, so they sat on the steps and in a few minutes the old gal came out with Arbuckle and a fresh-baked platter of doughnuts.

The old folks were named Davis and their spread was the Lazy D. The old man showed Longarm his grazing permit, signed by Latimer. Longarm nodded and said, "Mighty modest herd for this part of Texas, ain't it, Mr. Davis?"

Davis shrugged and said, "A hundred and fifty head is all one water tank and the prairie in reach of it will carry, Deputy Long. Me and old Martha, here, make do. The price of beef is rising and we've been breeding up our stock with a white-face he-brute. Want to see him? Naturally, we keep our prize stock penned out back and feed 'em corn. Can't make silage outten prairie short-grass, you know."

"I've noticed that. I'll pass on looking at your stock, sir. I've got more riding to do, as soon as I whup these fine doughnuts down to size. But as long as we're talking, I wonder if you'd mind answering some more questions."

"Fire away, son. Me and old Martha got nothing to hide."

"I figured as much. That's why your word's more important to me. I told you I was looking into the past doings of the late Hiram Latimer. When you paid him for your grazing permit, did you pay in cash or by check?"

148

"Writ out a check, of course," the old man said. "Ain't got the last few back from the bank, yet. But I can show you my stubs. Martha, dear, would you mind fetching me my checkbook from the desk inside?"

She said she'd be proud to and by the time Longarm had inhaled another doughnut she was out again to hand it to her husband.

He handed it to Longarm. "Third or fourth stub down," he said.

Longarm looked and, sure enough, he found a stub made out to the land office.

He noted the bank, check number, and the modest amount in his notebook before handing the checkbook back. Then he frowned and said, "Let me see that date again, Mr. Davis. You say you haven't gotten your canceled check back from the bank yet?"

"I haven't, and it's a funny thing," Davis said, "for I've gotten back some canceled checks I wrote *after* I paid Latimer this year. I wrote to my bank about it and they said not to worry. Since the check was never cashed yet, the money's still in my account."

"I'm worried about it, dear heart," old Martha Davis said. "I told you I didn't like the sneaky look in that land agent's eye."

"I know what you told me, Martha. Heard worse things about him in town, too. But what could he have been trying to pull on us? We paid for the grass, the cows are eating the grass, and the money's still in the bank drawing interest. Seems to me if anyone's ahead it's us. Don't you agree, Deputy Long?"

Longarm said, "Well, since you got your permit, nobody else can bill you. But Latimer sure seemed to have a mortal fear of *money,* for some reason, considering he should have needed a lot more than they was paying him. Wait a minute— I think I have the answer. The check wasn't made out to Latimer, so he couldn't have cashed it if he'd aimed to. The reason the *land office* never cashed it was 'cause he never turned it in. Yeah, that works, but the rascal must have been packing one big mess of signed checks in his saddlebag by the time that train run him down. And said saddlebag is still *missing!*"

Davis asked, "What happens when you find it, then?"

"I thank you for the compliment, sir. I don't have the first notion of where to *look* for it! But to answer your question, if and when the checks turn up, they'll naturally be turned over to Latimer's office to be cashed. Uncle Sam will doubtless be delighted by the windfall. Meanwhile, as you said, you and all the others who bought grazing permits still have your money in the bank, drawing interest."

He washed down the last doughnut it would be polite to take with coffee. "This sure beats all. I'm convinced some crooks are messed up in this case. But I surely fail to see how there's any *profit* in whatever they're up to."

"You'll likely tell me I'm a silly old biddy for trying to play detective gal," Martha Davis said. "But can I offer a suggestion, Deputy Long?"

He nodded, and she went on. "Well, suppose someone didn't *want* one or more of those checks cashed?"

Longarm blinked and whistled in admiration. "You sure are a good detective gal, ma'am! That *works!* Some of these hardscrabble outfits paid sizeable grazing fees, even after lying about how many head they had. The price of beef is up *this* summer, but *last* summer it was down. So many an outfit is hanging on by its fingernails and credit, hoping to last till they sell their beef this fall."

Old Davis slapped his thigh. "By cracky, I see it now. I never knowed you was so smart, Martha! If a man had to buy grass, but didn't have the money in the bank, he might well have been tempted to write a bum check. Would a man get in much trouble bouncing a check off the U. S. government, Deputy Long?"

"I'd surely advise against doing such a thing. It's still a sort of slim motive for serious skulduggery, though. The penalties for even *attempted* murder beat being overdrawn at the bank."

"Hell, son, I've heard of men being murdered for a nice

150

pair of boots, and some of our neighbors are sort of rustic rascals."

Longarm said he'd keep that in mind. He thanked the Davises for their hospitality and rode on. As he rode, he read another wire. The police in Latimer's home town said they were scouting for old photographs of Latimer and suggested he send postage and such for their time and effort. He grimaced and decided he'd solve the case or die trying before he'd have time to wait for the pictures and, worse yet, dig up an overripe head to compare them with.

Chapter 14

After a long, dull day in the saddle, Longarm got back to town without having learned much more. He hadn't even gotten laid, and one old gal had sicced her dog on him. But he knew now that Latimer's saddlebag—wherever the hell it was—had contained over ten thousand dollars' worth of checks from this part of Texas alone. And the wayward land agent had been collecting along the north line of No Man's Land before coming down here without reporting in to his office in Denver.

He didn't hear the piano as he approached the saloon after bedding Paint down in the livery. As he cooled his hot innards with a schooner of beer, the barkeep said that Red Robin had left town suddenly and never said why. Longarm didn't offer to enlighten him. He still thought she'd lied and that her boss had caught her robbing the office the way he'd said at her trial. For he knew her too well now to mistake her for an innocent little working gal who'd gun a man before she'd lay him. But, what the hell, if she kept messing up, she'd wind up caught, and if she really meant what she said about going straight, he owed a break to a gal who played piano and screwed with such enthusiasm. He just hoped she wouldn't shoot anyone before she settled down.

The gambling man, Doc Piper, was sitting in the corner, fooling around with his marked cards. Longarm refilled his schooner, went over, and sat down to join the tinhorn, saying, "Don't want to play cards with you. But, seeing as we have the place to ourselves this early, I thought I'd keep you company."

Doc Piper said, "I know who you are, and I don't want to play cards with you either, Longarm. I heard what you did to a gambling man in the Silver Dollar up in Denver a spell back."

"Oh, that wasn't gambling, it was personal. I'm surprised to find you here, Doc. It was my understanding you worked the trains along this section."

"You heard right. I'll tell you the truth, since it's not federal and I'm too young to get pistol-whupped. I am staying here to let things cool down at the north end of the line. I got into a minor dispute the other night in Kansas, and I suspect the Texas air will be better for my health until we find out if the son of a bitch is going to pull through or not."

Longarm nodded. "I figured you for a sensible cuss. Were you aboard the train the night Hiram Latimer got hit by it?" he asked.

"I was. That's one thing the law can't accuse me of. Both the conductor and the car porter can tell you, if you check, that I was dealing stud in a private compartment that morning."

"Hell, I was hoping you might have seen a drunk staggering between cars in a blue shirt and checked pants."

The tinhorn shook his head and said, "Can't say as I did. To answer your next question, yes, I did look the other passengers over some as I was setting up to entice prosperous-looking marks. I never play with shabby types. They're just as likely to be poor losers, and it's not worth it if a mark has no real money on him."

Longarm nodded. "Then you'd have noticed a shabby-dressed passenger, if only to dismiss him, right?"

"I can do better for you than that. I knew Latimer by sight, for he drank in here a lot, and once, on learning that despite his shiftless looks he packed lots of money for the government, I tried to interest him in a little friendly game of three-card monte. But he was a drinker, not a betting man."

"That's the first decent thing I've heard about him. Are you sure he couldn't have been aboard—maybe passed out in another compartment?"

"The conductor could tell you that better than me. But I'd say you were sniffing at the wrong lamppost. The conductor took part in the investigation afterwards. He'd have remembered any passenger riding first class. There ain't that many on a given train."

He turned over a card and grimaced. "There were all sorts of coach passengers, dressed all sorts of ways. I wouldn't have made a mental note of an old army shirt. But I'd have remembered seeing Latimer, since I knew him." He thought for a moment and added, "Now that I'm going over it all again in my head, I do remember a couple of odd birds aboard that night. I bumped into this gent, accidental, and he acted surly as hell for a minute. I thought he was fixing to start up with me, and I don't mind saying it was a time for a man's life to flash before his eyes. Him and his sidekick both wore buscadero rigs, and it was two to one. But then his sidekick nudged him and muttered something about more important fish to fry. So that was that."

Longarm nodded and said, "I know the feeling. Did you have a look at the dead gunslicks up at Sad Sam's hardware store?"

"Yeah, and that's not them. The gunmen on the train never got off here in Hitchland. They stayed aboard the

154

train as the section crews swapped places. I got off, of course, and I heard about the accident a while later. Whoever them gunslicks was aboard the train, they couldn't have been after you *or* Latimer."

"I'm glad to hear that *every* hired gun in the country ain't after me. You may be right if they went on down the line. Have you seen Pop Weddington of late?"

"Saw him about half an hour ago, making his rounds."

Longarm nodded his thanks and got to his feet to wait over at the bar. A beer later, a man dressed cow bellied up beside him and asked if he was Longarm. Longarm nodded to the stranger. "I'm the ramrod of the Slash Bar Seven," the cowboy said. "I hear there's something funny going on about our grazing permit." He took it out and spread it on the mahogany for Longarm to read.

Longarm said, "Well, she's signed by Latimer, and it says you paid for running five hundred head on government land. I don't reckon you'll get caught if it's no more than a thousand head. Latimer was supposed to look into things like that, but he don't seem to be on the job no more. And, what the hell, you'll be selling any day now."

The ramrod put the permit away and said that in that case he meant to buy Longarm a beer. Longarm said he'd pass. He heard a train whistle in the distance, and if Pop Weddington would be anywhere in town, it would be at the depot, staring suspiciously at the people getting off.

Longarm was right. As he joined the older lawman on the platform, the southbound locomotive hissed to a stop. All that got off was the mail sacks and a big husky gal with an awesomely corseted waistline and a big, husky hat. She spied Pop's badge and asked to be directed to the saloon. Pop said he'd be proud to carry her there. He told Longarm, "There's a couple of gents in my office asking about you, Longarm. I said I'd send you by when I met up with you. They're lawmen, by the way."

Longarm nodded and said he'd find out what they wanted. He knew the gal would be at the saloon later. She looked to be either the new piano player or a mighty serious drinker.

155

No other gal would be heading for a men's saloon at this hour.

Pop had been right about the two lawmen at his office being anxious to see Longarm. They wore deputy sheriff's badges that weren't any good in Texas unless they could prove they were in hot pursuit of somebody who'd acted awful north of the line.

He offered to shake, but they just stared soberly.

The older one said, "This is sort of awkward, Longarm, but a lady named Harris has laid some mighty serious charges at your door. Sheriff said we'd best see what you had to say for yourself."

"Do tell?" Longarm frowned, thinking back. Then he sighed. "I might have known. What's she trying to charge me with—rape or murder?"

"Both, with horse theft throwed in. She rode north to the county seat, looking mighty disgruntled, and swore out a warrant on you. Sheriff thought she was loco, seeing who she told her story on. But when we rode out to her stud spread, we found a couple of dead men buried right where she said we would. She said they'd been passing by as you was attacking her, so she couldn't say who they might have been. As they tried to save her, you gunned 'em both, knocked her out, and lit out with one of her best ponies."

His partner asked, "What have you got to say for yourself?"

"She made the horse up out of pure air, likely to account for one she sold without making out a bill of sale," Longarm said. "The other details are sort of bending the truth. I never discuss what I might or might not have done with a lady, but I will say I found no reason to rape her. She was sort of anxious to be pals."

He filled them in about the shootout and others he seemed to have been getting into a lot of late. When he'd brought them up to date, the older one scowled and said, "That's a mighty convincing tale, Longarm, and I know your rep with the ladies as well as in gunplay. But, damn it, why on earth would a woman make up a story like that? Could she have wanted revenge for your leaving her lovelorn on the prairie?"

"I ain't *that* special, boys. It was revenge she had in mind, now that I study on some suspicions I set aside before as having little to do with the more serious case I'm working. Since you know the Spooky Widow Harris you likely recall the story of her widowhood, right?"

"Sure. Her husband was killed a while back by a person or persons unknown."

"He ain't unknown no more. I gunned him the other night after he tried to set fire to my shirt tails. If you have a survey map handy I'll mark the spot so's you can pick up the remains, or just leave 'em out in the ashes. I don't care either way."

The older one took out his pocket map. "How do you figure this gent you shot so recent gunned the widow's man long before you could have been about to watch?" he asked.

Longarm spread the map on Weddington's desk and penciled in where he'd had the fight. "I'm good at putting two and two together," he said. "When I first joined the widow in her soddy, a man's cigar butt still smouldered on her table. She said she smoked cigars herself, but I never saw her do so. A man afoot in brush country can hide pretty good from a man aboard a bronc. So her lover must have lit out and hunkered down to give her time to get rid of me.

"He must have been wanted serious by the law. When she found out I was a federal lawman she worked so hard to convince me we was pals that I ought to be ashamed of myself. She tried to lure me away from my guns in a way I'd rather not talk about, and she would have had me set up nice for her armed boyfriend skulking in the brush had not some other gents come along who wanted my head on a platter, too. *Them's* the ones I told you about shooting it out with. *Next* time I come out of the house I was armed and dangerous again. I guess he run in the house to see if she was all right. He must have took what she told him jealous-hearted, for he sure followed me determined as hell."

"On foot?"

"Sure. How else would you follow a mounted man armed with a Winchester, if you'd just watched him use it good? Like I said, he was mad as a wet hen and likely sort of tuckered when he finally made his move. He lost, as old Betty could have told him he might, instead of blubbering it wasn't her fault that she'd all but raped me. Ain't it a bitch how some women get second thoughts after they cool down? Naturally, when he never come back, she *really* got mad at me. More important, she had a lot to cover up, and she didn't know what had happened to her lover boy. So she rode into town to charge me, to account for the bodies buried on her property, and to find out if your sheriff knew anything else. The rest ought to be emerging from the mists for you by now."

The lawman shook his head. "You must have keener eyes than us, Longarm. I believe you up to a point. But 'fess up. You're just making an educated guess that the lover she was hiding out on the sly was the man who gunned her husband, right?"

Longarm grinned sheepishly and said, "Yeah, you caught me. But it's still a mighty good guess, and it fits. A gal as mean as I now know her to be would surely be capable of covering her husband's murder. What do you want? You got motive, opportunity, and a bad habit of telling fibs to the law. Some damned body shot her man. Who fits better than an owlhoot she was hiding out and sleeping with?"

"Yeah, but how in hell would we ever prove that in court, Longarm?"

"Get her to confess, of course. By now she's probably already having second thoughts about such serious charges against a reasonably respectable peace officer. She's a mighty impulsive gal who's given to changes of mood when she calms down between 'em. She don't know what happened to her boyfriend. Suppose you found him, searching for me, and he made a sort of dying confession, blaming her for more than she really did?"

The two deputies exchanged glances, then the older one

laughed. "That's so dirty it has to *work!* I'm beginning to see how you've made such an impressive arrest record, Longarm. You lie worse than most of the crooks we catch."

They shook on it and he sent them on their way. Pop Weddington came in to confirm that the big gal in the big hat was indeed the new entertainer at the saloon, if they hired her. She'd heard about the job being open and came right down from Caldwell to ask about it. "I think she likes you, Longarm," Pop said. "She asked me who you was and descripted you as that nice-looking stud. Ain't that a bitch?"

Longarm said he was swearing off women, for a true one could seldom be found. He brought the older lawman up to date on his misadventure with the Spooky Widow Harris. Pop found the tale amusing and agreed that any sheriff worth his salt would surely trick a confession out of such a predictably unpredictable sass. "I'd say you was ahead, there, Longarm," he said. "You not only got some slap and tickle outten a pretty gal, nasty-hearted or not, but you just accounted for at least one gun who was trying to stop you from getting here."

Longarm said, "Yeah. Now if only I can figure out who sicced all them *other* guns on me, I'd feel even better!"

Chapter 15

The piano was playing again when Longarm bellied up to the bar in the saloon down the street. The new gal sure played in a different style from the way Red Robin had. He'd never heard "The Camptown Races" played so slow and sad. He admired her view from the back as she sat down at the end of the saloon. She was wasp-waisted, but she filled more of the piano bench than Red Robin had. Her hair turned out to be light brown and flowed down her back, now that she'd hung up her hat in Red Robin's former digs and unpinned her bun. He wondered if she knew "Jeannie with the Light Brown Hair." He decided not to ask her to play it. It would likely take her all night to play a song that started out slow.

The same ramrod for the Slash Bar Seven he'd talked to before came in, chaps flopping and wiping his face with his bandanna. He looked like he'd ridden hard through the dust and heat outside. But it would soon be cooling off, so Longarm smiled at him and said, "You'd better have a beer on me, right away. Hard day in the saddle?"

"That's for damn sure. Brush gets higher ever' summer, and we sure could use some rain. Feller just rode down out of the strip and when he stopped at the Slash Seven he said the bed of Beaver River's bone-dry out in the middle."

Longarm frowned. "I disremember crossing any *rivers* getting here," he said. "Rode across many a wash and draw, but I must have missed your Beaver River entirely."

"You couldn't have," the ramrod said. "Beaver River runs west to east, smack down the middle of the unassigned strip. Leastways, it do when the water table's higher. Its headwaters is seeps, over to the west, closer to the mountains."

Longarm signaled the barkeep for two schooners and listened to the piano a spell as he thought back on his long, tedious ride. Finally he said, "Well, I do mind a stretch of dry, flat sand as might have been a stream bed once. Ain't no fishing there *now*. It only stands to reason that if you put up enough windmills and overgraze in a dry year, the country has to dry up. You boys aiming to drive your market herd across No Man's Land this fall?"

"Not hardly. We'll poke 'em aboard here in Hitchland. Hardly anyone runs Texas cows north these days on foot, if they can prove they *own* 'em!"

Longarm chuckled and said he figured as much.

The ramrod took a healthy swig of beer before he said laconically, "I got a funny item in the mail this morning. Didn't you say you knew something about the land office?"

"Not as much as I started out thinking I did. Why?"

"They sent us a bill. Said we hadn't paid our range fee this year."

"Didn't you show me your permit a spell back?"

"I did. Want to see her again?"

"Not hardly. I remember reading her over this very bar. You're in the clear. Sometimes the right hand don't know

161

what the left hand is up to. But even the U. S. government can't bill you twice for the same thing."

"Even so, they *done* it! What would you do about it if you was me?"

"Nothing. I'll make a note that I saw your permit and I'll mention it when I get back to the land office, once I find out what happened to a certain saddlebag. I think I see what must have happened. Agent Latimer issued you a proper permit, but since his office never got your check, they don't have you on the books as paid up. By the way, you'd know if that check had ever been cashed, wouldn't you?"

"Sure. It ain't. Got a bank statement from Amarillo just the other day."

"Slash Bar Seven banks down in Amarillo?"

"Sure. Business account, of course. Makes the boss sleep easier to know all his funds ain't in a bitty crossroads bank any kid with a toy gun could rob. Why are you so interested in the Slash Bar Seven's bank account, Longarm?"

"I ain't, directly. I've established that different outfits bank in different banks. Some paid Latimer with business checks, some with personal checking accounts. At least one outfit told him to go to hell. Nobody, to date, reports paying him in cold cash."

"Then there couldn't have been much real cash on him when he got run over by that train, right?"

"He didn't even have any checks or I.O.U.'s aboard his carcass when they found him. Are you sure there's no standing water out in No Man's Land?"

"Not this time of the year. Not fit to drink. Why?"

"It's forty miles across. His horse never showed up on this side of the line. I can see a pony throwing a drunken rider. I can't see it wandering forty miles from water packing a stock saddle and all a man's gear."

"Yeah. The reins would be dragging, too. But try her this way. There's occasional travelers out in the unassigned lands. Some may be sort of avoiding contact with us more

162

law-abiding, civilized folk. There's Injun drifters from the Nation to the east. Injuns wander most ever' where, drunk or sober. Suppose someone found Latimer's pony, bushed from running, and just added her to his remuda?"

Longarm took a sip of beer and said, "That works. An outlaw would know better than to try to cash a check made out to Uncle Sam. An Indian might even use paper he couldn't read to start a campfire. I've met few Indians who don't know the value of *money* at this late date, but hand-writ checks might be over some folk's heads."

The ramrod asked, "What happens to all of us if the checks we wrote are lost forever, Longarm?"

Longarm opined, "I'd say you were all ahead a year's grazing fee. Whether said checks are ever cashed or not, you all got written receipts from a federal agent. You may get pestered some by sissy burro-cats. Hell, you're sure to get a mess of dunning letters, if that saddlebag's never found. But, like I said, nobody can make you pay again."

He frowned thoughtfully and added, half to himself, "Even a man who wrote a *bum check* is off the hook by now. He counted mentally, and groaned, "Oh, Jesus."

"What's the matter, Longarm? You look like you swallered a hair in your beer just now."

"I wish that was it. I'm used to doing legwork, but this is getting ridiculous! You stockmen bank all over creation. Some banks won't hand out information on their customers without a court order. I could take a month of Sundays checking out each and every bank account to find out who might have been overdrawn when they wrote Latimer a check. They could have brought their balance up to snuff by the time I *got* to 'em, too! There has to be an easier way!"

The ramrod thanked Longarm for the drink, said he was glad it wasn't his problem, and left.

The saloon was almost empty for the moment. It was just as well, for the gal at the piano was giving a mournful rendition of "Rally 'Round the Flag" now. Longarm walked over to her and said, "No offense, ma'am, but we're in Texas."

She went on playing as she looked up at him with a puzzled smile. Her face was sort of plump, too, but otherwise pretty.

"Texas was on the *other side* in the War Between the States, ma'am," he told her. "I can see it was before your time. You must have been a baby when Texas rode in butternut gray. But some old boys have long memories and short fuses. So I wouldn't play Yankee marching songs down here, even that slow."

"Heavens, I didn't even know the title of the tune," she said. "It's just a pretty old thing I remember hearing as a girl. I play by ear, you see."

"I figured as much, ma'am. I can see your kin rode for the North, too."

She told him she could see that he was smart, and said her name was Olive O'Shay. He told her who he was. She said Pop Weddington had told her as much. Before she could invite him to sit down at her side and teach her some Texas tunes, another gent came in flapping his chaps and waved a yellow telegram at Longarm. "They asked me to run this over to you, Deputy," he said. "Western Union says it looks important, and they figured you was likely here."

Longarm excused himself and moved back to the bar to read the wire privately as Olive commenced to play "Up in a Balloon" a lot differently from the way Red Robin had. He wondered if she was different in other ways from Red Robin. But when he read the wire, he saw that he'd never find out, if he did what Billy Vail said.

The Denver office wanted him home pronto. Vail said he'd added up all the things they'd found out between them and he was ready to write Latimer off as tolerably solved. They'd found out why he'd never reported back.

Mr. Waterford, down the hall, had said that the government could write off the missing checks if they never turned up. Lots of fees and taxes never got paid, but the U. S. A. took in enough to keep going, so what the hell.

Billy said that as Longarm had accounted for at least one of the men out to kill him, the others had likely had personal reasons, too. He asked why Longarm was making mountains out of molehills when there were plenty of more serious chores waiting for him back in Denver.

Longarm put the wire away to study on later. His boss made sense. That was more than anyone around here could offer. Every lead he'd followed had ended in a blind alley. Perhaps he was seeing a pattern in the wallpaper that nobody else had intended. Vail's theory worked, and it wasn't as if he *owed* anything to Latimer. He'd never met the cuss and from what he'd learned of him, he hadn't missed much. The man had been a sloppy bookkeeper, a shiftless drunk, and, if he hadn't been killed one way, he would likely have died another. Sad Sam Dillon had said his liver was already half gone when the train wheels chopped him up that night.

Pop Weddington came in, bellied up next to Longarm, and said, "Howdy. Ain't that gal playing 'Marching Through Georgia'?"

"Yeah, but don't pay her no mind. She's a Yankee gal, but she couldn't have ridden against Texas. It looks like we're about to part, Pop. My office wants me home. Boss says we've dead-ended a mighty tedious investigation."

"Well, we'll miss you, but I ain't surprised. I told you right off there wasn't much mystery to a drunk getting run over by a train. You told me about that fireman. I still say it's more likely he's what he denies being. Hardly any queers admit their unrulesome habits to the law, you know. Besides, no matter how it happened, it happened."

"Yeah. Doc Piper said Latimer couldn't have been aboard the train, as the fireman suggested. By the way, I don't see the gambling man about."

"Oh, that's no mystery. He went back up the line. Western Union says he picked up a message this morning. They must have told him it was safe to enter Kansas again."

Pop ordered two drinks. "I got an interesting wire on one of them boys we shot it out with the other night," he added. "Don't never get tattooed if you mean to change your name. His name was Quinn. They called him Killer Quinn, and with good reason. He was a gun for hire. No reward on him, sad to say. Son of a bitch was too professional."

Longarm frowned. "And they was *waiting* for someone here in Hitchland. It wasn't Latimer. He was already dead. It wasn't you or Doc Piper. You were both alive when I rode in. Unless they were waiting for Miss Olive over yonder, which don't seem likely, who's left?"

"I follows your drift. Ain't nobody from hereabouts they wouldn't have met afore you got here, and they wasn't aiming at you by the telegraph office because you'd insulted their mothers."

Longarm swallowed some beer. It read more than one way. As Billy Vail suggested, and as he'd sometimes discovered the harder way, a man in his line of work picked up personal enemies the way a dog picks up fleas. But how had they known he was coming to this bitty trail town?

That had a couple of answers, too. They could have been here on other business, spotted him, and decided to settle an old score for some pal he'd arrested or worse in his time. If hired guns had been after anyone else in Hitchland, they'd have gunned him, unless running into Longarm had upset their other plans before the mystery victim came in for a beer.

He grimaced as he saw that he was running his head in circles. "Well, I'll give it another day or so," he said. "By now everyone knows I'm here and still alive. If anyone's sicced gunslicks on me, this is as good a place to meet 'em as any. I'm forted good upstairs at night. You and your deputies are keeping an eye out for strange faces in a mighty small town. It beats camping out alone and hoping a pair of fool mares might warn me in time if professionals are moving in on me from the dark."

Pop said. "That's what I'd do, if I was you. But were you figuring on riding back?"

"Far as Trinidad. Why?"

"You'd make better time with you and the ponies going by rail. I know it's outten your way one hell of a ways, but trains go a hell of a lot faster. Why don't you just ride up Hutchinson, Kansas, and take the Santa Fe from there?"

"Makes sense, now that I've drug my ass this far east. I thank you for the notion, Pop. It gives me more time here in Texas without making my boss sore, too."

Olive was playing a sad dirge he didn't know now. Pop consulted his watch, said a southbound train was due in and asked Longarm if he wanted to come along and see if any spooky folks got off. Longarm declined, so Pop Weddington left on his own.

Longarm slid his beer schooner down the bar to where he'd have a sporting chance against anyone coming through the batwing doors. He wasn't really expecting anyone spooky to get off in a strange town at sunset. Professionals made a habit of arriving less conspicuously. Besides, by now, anyone who'd been trying to prevent him from learning something in Hitchland would assume he already had. Gunning him now would only confirm any suspicions he would have already wired to Billy Vail if only he wasn't so dumb.

He sipped his beer slowly. As time wore on the schooner got low and the fat bartender, Malone, drifted down to ask if he needed a head on it. Longarm said he was fine.

Malone chuckled and said, "We don't make much on gents who nurse their drinks. Only gent I ever saw taking as long to finish a beer was that land agent, Latimer—the one as got kilt."

Longarm frowned. "Do tell? The undertaker said he'd drunk his liver into awful shape."

Malone shrugged. "Well, some gents are like that. They can pile away awesome amounts of liquor for a spell and then drink sensible for a time. He did drink *steady*, as I recall. But now that I study on it, he drank a lot like you're drinking now. Like he was just killing time, waiting for something more interesting to happen."

"Do tell? How serious was he drinking the night he got killed?"

"Can't say, for sure," Malone said thoughtfully. "Don't even remember if he was *in* here that evening. Had other things on my head. We had us some ornery customers and I was keeping an eye on them."

"Fill me up again and tell me about 'em," Longarm said.

As Malone worked the beer tap he told a tale of hardcased strangers dressed cow and talking war. Actually one had been talking about gunning some son of a bitch and his pards were trying to simmer him down, as they all had more to drink than they should have. Longarm decided to file it away for the time being. There was an asshole in every outfit who talked war every time he'd had a few drinks.

He heard the train whistle outside. If nothing interesting happened in the next few minutes, nothing would. There were no other trains due before midnight, and he was damned if he was going to stay forted in this corner all night. He kept one eye on the door as he listened to Olive O'Shay play sad music nearby and he noticed she shot him a look from time to time, too. He didn't plan ahead on just how he'd work it, but at closing time they'd have the whole building to themselves, and she'd already confessed that she sort of admired him. If she was interested at all he didn't have to study too hard on who'd say what when to whom. If she wasn't, there wasn't anything he could do about that, either. A man just had to leave things up to sad, quiet gals. He'd found they did their own seducing.

Chapter 16

For a gal who played piano so slowly, Olive sure moved her body with considerable enthusiasm, and she had a lot of body to move. She looked even plumper once she took her duds and corset off, but she was reasonably pretty, and the nice thing about a gal with a big rump was that a man didn't need a pillow under it to present her front entrance at a welcoming angle.

After they'd gotten to know one another better, they took a break to share a cheroot and tell each other the tales of their lives as she snuggled against him, filling the narrow bed almost to overflowing.

As he'd suspected, Olive was from the north part of back East, where she'd heard lots of Yankee marching songs as a child, but she hadn't taken them personally. Her immigrant daddy had timed his birthday right to miss the draft. She was a sweet little thing—or, perhaps more accurately, a sweet big thing—and if she had much going in the way of brains, it wasn't too evident.

She'd been used and abused by life about as much as any dumb, pretty gal who admired men but considered it improper to lay them for money. She'd run into Red Robin up the line and, as professional entertainers helped each other out the same as hobo gents, Red Robin had told her there was a vacant piano bench here in Hitchland. As she fondled Longarm's pecker, Olive said she was sure glad she'd applied for the job. She'd found Hitchland a right friendly town so far.

He listened to her prattle on mostly to be polite as he enjoyed a smoke while trying to build up a head of steam for more of her more interesting charms. So the first time she said it, it almost passed over him. He frowned and asked, "What was that about a bum check again, honey?"

"I told you," she said. "That mean-hearted rascal in Kansas City left us all stranded when he slickered us with paychecks we couldn't pass. The Kansas City law said we couldn't charge him with a felony, even if we caught up with him some day, because of the slick trick he'd pulled. It's against the law to write a check on a bank you don't have money in, but it's not against the law to make a *mistake* writing out a check. And if the check's written wrong, the bank won't cash it. They said the rascal had opened a valid account with 'em and that if we all caught up with him and made him write our checks out right, some of 'em would no doubt bounce like rubber balls. But there was enough in the account to cover maybe one or two checks and since we couldn't cash *any* of 'em..."

"I see that part. What did he do that made the checks uncashable?"

"He used stock bank checks and wrote the wrong account number in the little squares under his signature. How on earth were any of us to know what his account number was? The checks *looked* good. He paid us on a weekend when the bank was closed, and one cold gray Monday morning, after he was long gone..."

"I can see how he wrote you goldbricks," Longarm said absently as he snuffed out his cheroot. Her fondling was starting to inspire him to more pleasant huffing and puffing again. Olive saw that he was no longer in a mood for idle conversation and commenced to kiss her way down his body, tickling him like a kitten with her pointed pink tongue. As she raised her considerable rump to crawl down further and lower her rosebud lips to the tip of his organ grinder, Longarm suddenly blinked and gasped. "Son of a bitch! That's *it!*"

She stopped what she'd started. "What's wrong, darling man?" she asked. "Don't you like French loving?"

"Oh, you just go ahead with that pretty head, little darling. I wasn't calling *you* a son of a bitch. I was calling *me* a son of a bitch for being so *dumb* all this time. I should have seen it right off!"

She couldn't talk with her mouth full, so Olive swiveled around, got one of her plump knees on opposing edges of the mattress with Longarm's hips between them, and settled down to sigh contentedly as she impaled herself on him. "What on earth are you talking about, dear?" she asked.

He couldn't thrust enough to matter with a gal that fat on his lap, but he managed to move enough to inspire her as he explained. "Your tale of improperly made out checks jogged the penny loose in the slot of my brain it was stuck in. I know now what they were afraid I'd stumble over as I wandered about pestering folks. The hell of it was, I never *would* have if they hadn't kept reminding me there had to be more to this case than a worthless bill collector falling drunk under a train one night in the dark. I'm a man of action, not a paper wrangler."

Olive giggled and said she was a gal of action, too, as she started bouncing up and down, imperiling the bed-springs. She was a mite shorter than Longarm, but she weighed as much or more. He'd been known to bust through to the floor with his weight spread out more in a moment of pure passion. So he suggested they swap places to do it right.

She giggled again and got off, winding up on her feet as she implored him to hurry. He rose, too, but before lowering her to the bed again he took her in his arms to kiss her romantic, standing up as well as stark. Olive was built long-legged and by bending his knees slightly he could fit his erection between her marshmallow thighs. She tongued him as she held him about the waist and started thrusting with her hips, enjoying the novelty of their new position by sliding back and forth the length of his shaft.

He moved her back a few steps to brace her against the panels of the locked door as he bent his knees a mite more, reached down with one hand, and tried to guide it in right. She sensed what he had in mind and, still kissing, rose on the toes of her bare feet to help. She tilted her pelvis toward him, there was an awkward moment of moist, soft, but unyielding pressure, and then, with a delicious pop, he was in her to the hilt.

She started rolling her head back and forth across the door panel, gasping. Olive was so padded that it didn't bother her to be pounded against the solid wood of the old cathouse crib door. But the lock wasn't as strong as it might have been, and the next thing they knew, the door crashed open and the two of them fell full length on the rug of the hall outside.

He gasped, "Are you hurt?" in a worried tone. For, though he was still in her, they'd shaken the whole building falling together.

Olive giggled. "I think I'll live. But, my God, you sure work hard to touch bottom, cowboy!"

He moved experimentally in her and chuckled. "Yeah, but I don't feel any broken bones, or anything else that might have been busted, considering."

She cradled him in her soft flesh and responded to his thrusts. "Don't you think we'd better get back inside, dear?" she panted.

"Not just now. There's nobody in the building but us. We got all night and a whole saloon to ourselves."

Olive saw the wisdom in his words and got into the spirit of the rare opportunity by making a shocking suggestion. So, after they'd come on the rug upstairs, they went downstairs hand in hand like a pair of naked, giggling kids and shared some Maryland rye as he laid her again atop the mahogany bar. The nice thing about a well-padded gal was that a man could lay her almost anyplace.

But when Olive suggested he do her dog style as she played the piano, he told her she was being silly. He could see how a piano-playing gal could cook up such a fantasy, sitting night after night with her rump aimed at a saloon full of men. But, as he told her when they did it on the bar some more instead, there were limits to what even free thinkers like them could get away with. And piano playing in a bitty trail town at three in the morning wasn't one of them.

Olive said she'd never forget Longarm when they parted friendly the next morning. She'd likely remember him at least until roundup time, when things got less tedious in Hitchland. He never told Pop Weddington what he'd figured out about the case, but he took Pop's advice on getting back to Denver by the longer but quicker route. He neglected to tell Billy Vail that he was coming, or anything else. He wasn't being negligent. He wanted to see what happened when he had it narrowed down to where only one set of folks knew his timetable. Everyone in Hitchland knew the time he and his ponies boarded the northbound combo. So, when nothing much went wrong on the way to Denver, he verified his hopes about the old lawman being straight and the folks of Hitchland mostly innocent fools, like *he'd* been.

They rolled into Denver yards late in the afternoon. Longarm didn't notify his office he was back. He took the ponies out to the Diamond K and they accepted his explanation about losing Browny once they saw what a natural cutting horse Buck was.

When they shook on it, Longarm asked the ramrod of

the spread for another favor. He said, "I'd take it neighborly if I could bunk out here tonight. Not in the bunkhouse. Hayloft would do me fine."

The ramrod frowned. "You're welcome to bunk any-wheres out here, save for with my or the owner's wives. But whatever happened to that room you hire over by Cherry Creek, Longarm? Forget to pay your landlady, or did you try to get in *her* bed, too?"

Longarm laughed. "Not hardly. My rent's paid, and my landlady's old and ugly. We get along, so she'd likely keep it a secret if I asked her not to tell anyone I was back in town. But it's a strain on a woman to hold her tongue, and the neighbors would be sure to notice even if I came over the back fence wearing a mask."

"I've warned my wife about discussing business at the general store. But how come you don't want nobody to know you're back?"

"If I told you, you'd know. I'm trying to narrow things down by not letting even my *friends* know what I'm up to. I have to trust you and your boys to keep it quiet that I'm back, but it can't be helped. I've got to stay somewhere tonight, and I'm sore as hell about it, too. I wasted a whole two meals on the train trying to make friends with a lady who was traveling alone, and now I daren't even settle my nerves with one of my old gal pals here in Denver."

"You could likely make it from here to a certain address on Sherman Avenue, Longarm. I hear the widow's relatives has left for the East again."

Longarm smiled wisfully and said, "That's my point entirely. If gents I only borrow a mount from now and again know about that brownstone house I sometimes frequent, anyone taking me more serious likely does, too. It's getting so a gent can hardly nod at a gal in Denver without them printing it in the infernal Post! Got some important arresting to do come daybreak, so I may as well rise bright-eyed and bushy-tailed after a good night's sleep alone."

He was awakened before dawn by the sound of flowers

and the smell of birds. The morning breeze off the Front Range was banging heavy sunflower heads against the side of the barn, and the chickens roosting under the hayloft smelled awful. He thought for a moment he was back with poor old Roping Sally, a gal who'd also kept chickens and sunflowers too close for comfort, although she'd been mighty comforting in other ways. Then he remembered Roping Sally was dead. So he swallowed the lump in his throat and skipped breakfast at the Diamond K. It was the last working day of the week and, if he didn't hurry, he could miss the son of a bitch he was out to pinch.

He caught a ride into Denver with a friendly produce farmer and got to the federal building even earlier than he'd timed his arrival. He went up the granite steps to pound the bronze doors and get the night watchman to let him in. But, as he was about to knock, he saw another gent in a business suit coming around the corner. He smiled grimly and turned to face the new arrival. The slightly older and skinnier gent nodded at Longarm and said, "My streetcar was ahead of time for a change, too. Don't I know you? You're one of Marshal Vail's deputies, aren't you?"

"I am," Longarm said. "I've seen you about the hallways, too, Mr. Waterford. I reckon you paid more attention to me than I did to you up to now."

Waterford looked nervously around, shrugged, and asked, "Well, don't you think we should go inside?"

"Door's locked. We could wake up the watchman, but my boss usually gets here early and they gave him his own key to keep from being so disturbed every morning. He should be along directly. But you ain't going to your office upstairs this morning, Waterford. You're going over to the federal lockup as soon as I explain why to old Billy Vail. You're under arrest."

Waterford tried to look surprised. "What are you talking about, Longarm? You can't arrest *me!*" he protested.

"Sure I can. I just did. You ain't wearing any serious guns and I can likely beat you to the draw if you're packing

175

a private derringer. So I'll stand here civilized as long as you do. Billy ought to be here most any minute, you son of a bitch."

Waterford glared and snapped, "I'll remember you called me that after we clear this ridiculous business up! Do you mean to just stand there cursing an unarmed man, or do you have some charge to make, Deputy?"

"Oh, hell, you know what you done. That's why I called you a son of a bitch. I'm an easygoing, live-and-let-live gent about lots of things. I see no call to fuss at folks who hold unusual views the law might nitpick as crimes against nature. I can overlook a missing bill of sale on livestock the U. S. government has no claim on. I can even overlook manslaughter, if a lady has a good excuse. But a public official who betrays the trust of the taxpayers by dipping his hand in the till is...Well, I already called you a son of a bitch and I won't strain my library of cusswords trying to come up with something more fitting. For there just ain't words to describe a man as low as you, Waterford!"

"I don't know what you're talking about. Are you drunk?"

"No. And neither was Hiram Latimer when you talked him into going along with your scheme. I sent some wires as I was leaving Hitchland. I picked up the answers in Kansas as I was changing trains. So I know you're fixing to retire, soon, and that you'd had orders from headquarters to fire Latimer if he messed up again. You called him in during one of his sober spells and explained how he'd never last with the man who replaced you. So he went along with your plan to bilk the land office."

"I still don't know what you're driving at, Longarm. You wired from Texas that Latimer was dead and buried."

"I know I did. I knew my poor, innocent boss was keeping you abreast of the case by the hour, too. That's why I told everyone to wire me care of the Hutchinson, Kansas Western Union. We both know Latimer never got run over by a train. The sweet young thing playing the typewriter upstairs told me that Latimer wore chaps. Everybody riding through that brush down there along the fringes of the un-

176

assigned lands wear chaps, save for strangers of the county like me and the drunk your boys dropped between the cars of a moving train that night. Nobody who knew Latimer remembered seeing him aboard said train, for the simple reason he was never aboard her. Your killers lured a hobo who looked sort of like Latimer aboard. It wouldn't have been hard, if they were offering to buy him drinks. They talked him into putting on Latimer's duds. They forgot *underwear*. But hardly anybody wondered how a man could ride in wool pants in high summer wearing no chaps or underwear. The duds identified the body tolerably, once it had been cut up and battered by the tracks and wheels. Folks in town who knew Latimer to nod to didn't look close as they said it was him. But the undertaker said his liver was so bad he was almost dead before you had him killed. So it wasn't Latimer. Latimer was a periodic drunk who could *hold* his liquor when he had more interesting things to do. Were you splitting fifty-fifty, or was he on shares like the rest of the gang, Waterford? By the way, your gang ain't as big as it started out, now. I'd say I got most of them, here and there in my travels."

"What gang are you talking about, you idiot? Do I look like a gang leader?"

"Nope. That's why my office was keeping you posted on my moves as I wandered into more than one ambush, Waterford. You slipped up there, or perhaps you didn't think I'd win, so it didn't matter. It didn't take me long to figure someone was *wiring my movements ahead*. I doubted like hell it was Billy Vail. So you, just down the hall, were the only other person who could have known where I was after I'd wired in a few changes of direction."

Waterford sneered. "You must be drunk. Assuming I was a busy little bee sending wires to outlaws all over creation, have you some *motive* to tell the grand jury about? Confess, Longarm, you're just fishing. You think you're being persecuted, and you're trying to blame me for the fact that you're simply not too popular."

Longarm saw there was time, since no other office workers seemed as anxious to get there early as Waterford had been. He said, "Well, at the risk of telling a man what he already knows, I'll tell you what I mean to tell the grand jury. You sent Latimer out to collect grazing fees."

"Of course I did, you fool! That's his job!"

"I ain't finished. You sent him over his usual route, along the north line to the unassigned strip. Then, being piggy, you sent him along the *south* line, too. It surprised hell out of the land office down Texas way, as they thought it was up to *them* to collect there. To save more dumb denials, I checked and, sure enough, there's a sometimes river dividing No Man's Land in halves, smack down the middle. Most years it's a treacherous, raging stream, and there's no ferryboats in uninhabited territory. Your range district don't *run* as far south as Texas line. But to most settlers, a land agent is a land agent. Half of 'em don't have much education. Latimer showed them how to write out their checks. Made out proper, range fees are made payable to the Bureau of Land Management, or just United States Government. The words land management or land office alone don't mean much—unless, of course, some slicker's set up a private realty corporation calling itself Land Management Incorporated, or just Land Office, period.

"It's a caution how casual folks are about naming things Federal Loan, Union this, or National that. The reason we never found the saddlebags of a missing land agent was that he'd brought 'em to you, stuffed with checks you was fixing to cash here in Denver at the bank you spend so much time at during business hours.

"I know you ain't done it yet, for you're still here. And none of the folks who thought they were buying grass have got their canceled checks back yet. Where are you hiding 'em? Your office safe upstairs, or at home? I can get a warrant to search both, and I mean to, once I turn you over to Billy."

Waterford shook his head as if in wonder and said, "You've created a whole dream world out of bits and pieces of unrelated facts, Longarm! I'll show you the contents of my safe upstairs, if we can go *in,* now. As for Latimer being alive or dead, on the right range or strayed, it's not *my* fault. Everyone knows he's not responsible."

"I thank you for saving me the bother of going through at least one hiding place. Latimer was responsible all right. You told him to be careful and he was. He never reported a man who refused to pay his grazing fee, like he would have if you hadn't told him he only had to make one last trip and not to draw any attention to himself. *You* didn't draw attention when he missed a couple of paydays. You said you didn't know his pay had been docked for a wife and kid he'd deserted back East. Alone, that could have been careless bookkeeping. Put it together with all the other odd habits you two rats seemed to have and I reckon the grand jury will buy it."

He smiled and added, "Here comes old Billy Vail now. We'll tie up any loose ends left between us as I write up my report."

Waterford turned, too, as Billy Vail came toward them on his short, stumpy legs. Vail blinked in surprise as he saw Longarm on the steps of the office ahead of starting time.

Waterford reached casually in his vest pocket. Longarm whipped out his own gun first and snapped, "Grab some sky, you slick bastard!"

Marshal Vail froze as he saw his deputy throw down on a fellow employee in the middle of what had seemed a friendly conversation. Then Vail's jaw dropped further as he stared past Longarm and yelled, "Custis! *Duck!*"

Longarm spun and ducked away from Waterford just as a bullet whizzed through the space he'd been. He fired into the gunsmoke of a man dressed shabby and cow as the bastard fired up at him again. The stranger's slug missed. Longarm's hit him just above his drinker's nose and crossed his eyes around the bullet tearing through his skull. Before the body hit the walk, Longarm spun back to see if Vail had Waterford covered.

The marshal had his own gun out and was moving up

the steps as Waterford crumpled at the knees and went down them ass-over-teakettle to wind up on the same walk as his confederate, staring dead at the sky.

Longarm started to reload as he observed laconically, "That's *one* way to save tedious paperwork. I confess all I had on Waterford was circumstantial until or unless I find the checks as solid evidence. Lucky for us, the rascals panicked. Lucky for *me*, you *noticed!* I owe you again, Billy. I sure feel foolish for never guessing today was the day they meant to meet here and settle up. I should have. It's the last banking day of the month, with a weekend coming."

Vail holstered his own weapon as a police whistle blew and men came running from all directions. "I don't know what you're talking about," Vail said. "I surely hope *you* do, for you just gunned an important public official, Longarm."

Longarm pointed his chin at the other body down the walk and said, "I never shot Waterford. I shot *that* son of a bitch as he put a round in his pard he'd meant for me. And if he ain't Hiram Latimer in the flesh, I sure don't study descriptions good, over and over. He was coming to meet his confederate. He saw us talking and hung back, puzzled, until he saw I was arresting the ringleader."

Longarm holstered his .44 and added, "He could have just faded back, if he'd had sense. I reckon he'd put so much effort into the swindle he lost his head when he saw Waterford's hands and his retirement plans going up in the pure blue sky together."

A Denver copper was standing over Latimer's corpse, staring up at them thoughtfully. Vail called down an explanation as the big bronze doors of the federal building opened and a worried-looking watchman peered out at them.

"Sorry we woke you up," Longarm said. "But as long as you're handy, go help that copper get them stiffs to the morgue. Come on, boss, we got to bust into an office without no warrant."

Vail said he was game. But as they went up the stairwell

of the deserted building, he kept asking pesky questions until Longarm had Vail well filled in. As Longarm picked the lock of Waterford's door, Vail asked, "Wouldn't it be simpler if I just had you check the banks here in town, old son? If he set up a dummy corporation, he must have left a paper trail, you know."

"I know, boss, but have you any notion of how *many* banks I'd have to walk through? He may have used an alias. Even if he presented his fool self under his right name as an officer of the company, we'd have to dig through papers indeed. The damned secret account would be made out in the company name, not his."

They went inside. Vail eyed the office safe soberly. "That's not a box you can open with a penknife, Longarm. There's a combination lock."

"I noticed. He said I was welcome to look in yon safe, too. So let's start with some less likely places."

They were going at it when Waterford's little secretary gal came in, stared at Longarm going through her desk and Vail pulling a picture off the wall, and demanded, "What are you gentlemen doing in Mr. Waterford's office?"

Longarm saw that she hadn't put a pencil in her bun yet, and she looked a mite prettier, early in the day. "This ain't Waterford's office no more, miss—what did you say your name was?"

"I'm Anita Lee and I'm Mister Waterford's personal secretary. And if I didn't know you *were* the law I'd call the law on you. What on earth are you looking for?"

"Range fees, Miss Anita. You'll be personal to another boss in a day or so, I reckon. But your late boss was a crook, and now he's dead. Tell you why later. Do you know the combination of this safe?"

"Of course. And it's where he kept private papers, too. But, for heaven's sake, what happened to him?"

"Open the safe. The case ain't quite closed, Miss Anita."

She blanched, dropped to her knees before the safe, and began to spin the dial. "Do you suspect *me* of anything?" she asked. "I swear I don't know what this is all about."

As she swung the heavy door open and moved aside, Longarm said, "I never said you did, Miss Anita. For one thing, you don't look dumb. So it couldn't have been the slip of a crooked gal's tongue when you mentioned Latimer wearing chaps after the gang knew he'd been replaced in a grave by a man *not* wearing any. You mentioned your boss going on a banking errand during business hours, too. He'd likely have had a fit had he known you gave that away, but he never, so no harm done."

"Do you know what bank he spent so much time in, Miss?" Vail asked.

Longarm started searching the safe drawers.

The brown-haired gal said, "He had two bank accounts. I asked him about that one time when they both mailed monthly statements. He got upset, told me to mind my own business, and went out. I know he cashed his paycheck at Colorado National, for so do I. The other bank was Drover's Trust, I think."

Vail wrote it down and thanked her. "Find anything, Longarm?" he asked.

Longarm lifted out a big metal drawer and placed it atop the safe. "I did, and he was a liar to the last. Look at this, boss!"

Vail and the girl joined him. They stared soberly down at a stockless sawed-off ten-guage resting on top of a drawer filled with sealed envelopes. Vail whistled as the girl said that was the drawer she'd been told never to open.

Longarm said, conversationally, "He was grasping at a last straw when he invited me up here to his office. Nobody was around. I don't think it would have worked, but he must have been desperate for such a cool-talking cuss."

Vail nodded and removed an envelope to open it. "A man who tried for a derringer standing betwixt the two of us must have had a lot on his conscience. Here's a check signed by a spider or a semi-literate named Davis. It's made out in more legible block lettering to Land Management Incorporated. Here's another written the same way."

Longarm said, "Yeah, they put down all sorts of things

on their own stubs in their own unsteady hands. But wasn't Latimer nice to make them range fee checks out so neat for one and all? He naturally added the *'Incorporated,'* after."

Vail opened another envelope and snorted. "Tell me things I can't see with my own two eyes. Shoot, here's more checks, made out in a dozen different pens and drawing on a dozen out-of-state banks. What I'm looking for is deposit slips."

Longarm grinned at Anita, since she was prettier, but addressed his boss. "You ain't awake yet, Billy. I know they'd have had to deposit them checks and wait for them to clear before they could draw cash for their unexpected retirement from an *honest* bank. But if Waterford had deposited all them checks, they wouldn't be here right now, and he wouldn't have been do desperate."

Vail smiled sheepishly. "All right, you caught me not thinking. But from here on the trail leads through pure paper. It's going to take a parcel of bank examiners to track down Waterford's confederate or confederates Drover's Trust."

The little secretary gasped. "Heavens, are those *bankers* crooks, too?"

"Maybe only one or two, ma'am," Longarm said. "Folks like us have to wait till our deposited checks clear before we can draw out cash. And even if we do, no teller's about to give us a satchel full of money all at once unless a *bank officer* says to."

Vail grimaced, tossed an envelope back in the drawer still sealed, and said, "As long as we have to turn all these misdirected range fees over to Uncle Sam for proper collection, I may as well deal the treasury men down the hall into the case now. We're peace officers, not bookkeepers. We got the gun-toting crooks. It could take weeks of nit-picking to find out if some bank officials were crooked or just stupid."

Longarm nodded, "I'd say any bank officials working with the ringleader, Waterford, were likely just greedy dupes, Billy. They could verify the checks by wire and authorize a sudden big withdrawal for a cash consideration. He wouldn't have told 'em that eventually, when said checks started returning by mail to the little folks who signed 'em . . ."

"I *said* I'd let *Treasury* do the nitpicking, old son," Vail said.

"The case is about wrapped, as far as Justice is concerned. But we still have some paperwork in our own office. You coming, Longarm?"

Longarm was smiling down at Anita again. She was blushing a becoming shade as Longarm replied. "You go on ahead and I'll join you directly, boss. I promised this young lady some full explaining, and it should only take me a few minutes to find out if she's forgiven me for being so interested in her drawers."

Watch for

LONGARM AND THE BIG OUTFIT

fifty-ninth novel in the bold
LONGARM series from Jove

coming in October!

LONGARM

Explore the exciting Old West with one of the men who made it wild!

_____	07524-8	LONGARM #1	$2.50
_____	06807-1	LONGARM ON THE BORDER #2	$2.25
_____	06809-8	LONGARM AND THE WENDIGO #4	$2.25
_____	06810-1	LONGARM IN THE INDIAN NATION #5	$2.25
_____	06950-7	LONGARM IN LINCOLN COUNTY #12	$2.25
_____	06070-4	LONGARM IN LEADVILLE #14	$1.95
_____	06155-7	LONGARM ON THE YELLOWSTONE #18	$1.95
_____	06951-5	LONGARM IN THE FOUR CORNERS #19	$2.25
_____	06627-3	LONGARM AT ROBBER'S ROOST #20	$2.25
_____	06628-1	LONGARM AND THE SHEEPHERDERS #21	$2.25
_____	07141-2	LONGARM AND THE GHOST DANCERS #22	$2.25
_____	07142-0	LONGARM AND THE TOWN TAMER #23	$2.25
_____	07363-6	LONGARM AND THE RAILROADERS #24	$2.25
_____	07066-1	LONGARM ON THE OLD MISSION TRAIL #25	$2.25
_____	06952-3	LONGARM AND THE DRAGON HUNTERS #26	$2.25
_____	07265-6	LONGARM AND THE RURALES #27	$2.25
_____	06629-X	LONGARM ON THE HUMBOLDT #28	$2.25
_____	07067-X	LONGARM ON THE BIG MUDDY #29	$2.25
_____	06581-1	LONGARM SOUTH OF THE GILA #30	$2.25
_____	06580-3	LONGARM IN NORTHFIELD #31	$2.25
_____	06582-X	LONGARM AND THE GOLDEN LADY #32	$2.25

Available at your local bookstore or return this form to:

JOVE
Book Mailing Service
P.O. Box 690, Rockville Centre, NY 11571

Please send me the titles checked above. I enclose _____
Include $1.00 for postage and handling if one book is ordered; 50¢ per book for
two or more. California, Illinois, New York and Tennessee residents please add
sales tax.

NAME _____

ADDRESS _____

CITY _____ STATE/ZIP _____

(allow six weeks for delivery)   5

LONGARM

Explore the exciting Old West with one of the men who made it wild!

___06583-8	LONGARM AND THE LAREDO LOOP #33	$2.25
___06584-6	LONGARM AND THE BOOT HILLERS #34	$2.25
___06630-3	LONGARM AND THE BLUE NORTHER #35	$2.25
___06953-1	LONGARM AND THE SANTA FE #36	$2.25
___06954-X	LONGARM AND THE STALKING CORPSE #37	$2.25
___06955-8	LONGARM AND THE COMANCHEROS #38	$2.25
___07412-8	LONGARM AND THE DEVIL'S RAILROAD #39	$2.50
___07413-6	LONGARM IN SILVER CITY #40	$2.50
___07070-X	LONGARM ON THE BARBARY COAST #41	$2.25
___07538-7	LONGARM AND THE MOONSHINERS #42	$2.50
___07525-6	LONGARM IN YUMA #43	$2.50
___07431-4	LONGARM IN BOULDER CANYON #44	$2.50
___07543-4	LONGARM IN DEADWOOD #45	$2.50
___07425-X	LONGARM AND THE GREAT TRAIN ROBBERY #46	$2.50
___07418-7	LONGARM IN THE BADLANDS #47	$2.50
___07414-4	LONGARM IN THE BIG THICKET #48	$2.50
___07522-1	LONGARM AND THE EASTERN DUDES #49	$2.50
___06251-0	LONGARM IN THE BIG BEND #50	$2.25
___07523-X	LONGARM AND THE SNAKE DANCERS #51	$2.50
___06253-7	LONGARM ON THE GREAT DIVIDE #52	$2.25
___06254-5	LONGARM AND THE BUCKSKIN ROGUE #53	$2.25
___06255-3	LONGARM AND THE CALICO KID #54	$2.25
___07545-0	LONGARM AND THE FRENCH ACTRESS #55	$2.50
___06257-X	LONGARM AND THE OUTLAW LAWMAN #56	$2.25
___06258-8	LONGARM AND THE BOUNTY HUNTERS #57	$2.50
___06259-6	LONGARM IN NO MAN'S LAND #58	$2.50

Available at your local bookstore or return this form to:

JOVE
Book Mailing Service
P.O. Box 690, Rockville Centre, NY 11571

Please send me the titles checked above. I enclose_____. Include $1.00 for postage and handling if one book is ordered; 50¢ per book for two or more. California, Illinois, New York and Tennessee residents please add sales tax.

NAME_____

ADDRESS_____

CITY_____ STATE/ZIP_____

(allow six weeks for delivery.)

6